WILD RESCUERS
EXPEDITION
ON THE
TUNDRA

And don't miss

Wild Rescuers: Guardians of the Taiga
Wild Rescuers: Escape to the Mesa

WILD RESCUERS

EXPEDITION ON THE TUNDRA

Stacy Hinojosa aka *Stacy Plays*

ILLUSTRATED BY Vivienne To

HARPER
An Imprint of HarperCollinsPublishers

Photos on pages 165–166 courtesy of StacyPlays
Photos on pages 167–172 courtesy of Wes Larson

Wild Rescuers: Expedition on the Tundra
Text copyright © 2020 by Stacy Plays LLC
Map illustration copyright © 2020 by Virginia Allyn
Interior illustrations copyright © 2020 by Vivienne To
Rune illustrations by Madeline Lansbury, © 2020 by Stacy Plays LLC

Library of Congress Control Number: 2019956221
ISBN 978-0-06-296074-0 — ISBN 978-0-06-298377-0 (special edition)
Typography by Jessie Gang
20 21 22 23 24   PC/LSCH   10 9 8 7 6 5 4 3 2
❖
First Edition

For Nan

CONTENTS

WILD RESCUERS
EXPEDITION
ON THE
TUNDRA

the arctic fox den

the ice floes

SOUTH
to Taiga

Stacy

Everest

Wink

Basil

Tucker

Addison

Noah

Page

Milquetoast

Molly

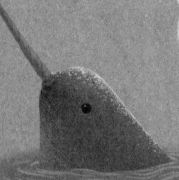

Norman

Polar Bear

Arctic Fox

Pipsqueak

ONE

"HHHEELLLPPPP!" STACY SHOUTED at the top of her lungs. She was sliding down a steep mountainside, helpless against the avalanche that had carried her away from her wolf pack moments earlier.

Suddenly, everything around her stopped moving. She was trapped in the stillness—suspended in the snow, unable to tell which way was up or down. An eerie calm rushed over her . . . and then fear. The avalanche had subsided, and she hadn't been carried off a cliff or broken any bones. But her current situation was worse—she had been buried under at least thirty feet of snow and would run out of oxygen in minutes . . . maybe even less.

I'm going to die, Stacy thought to herself. *We're going to die.* She reached down into her satchel and stroked the lynx kitten's tiny head. It stirred, too weak to do much else, and Stacy could feel the vibrations of its purrs against her fingertips. A tear crept out of the corner of one of Stacy's eyes and froze on her cheek. She closed her eyes and thought of the happiest memory she could. It was two weeks ago, back in the taiga in the clearing outside of their cave, before they decided to journey to the tundra, before she knew about the elder wolves, before any of this had happened. . . .

"Three . . . two . . . one! Okay, ready or not, here I come!" Stacy opened her eyes and looked around the clearing. None of her wolves or Page were in sight, but Molly—the littlest and newest member of her pack—was sitting at her feet, staring up at her with a quizzical expression. Her head was cocked to one side, and her giant floppy ears hung like pigtails on either side of her white-and-brown-spotted face.

"I guess you don't understand hide-and-seek, do you, girl?" Stacy said, reaching down to pat the small beagle on the head. "We need to go find the others . . . come!" That was a command Stacy was at least pretty sure the little dog knew. She'd only had Molly for about three months, but it was clear Molly's previous owners hadn't taught her many commands. They'd obviously not cared for her at all, which is how Molly had wound up lost and stranded on a ledge in the mesa biome, which is where Stacy and her pack of wolves had rescued her. But whatever Molly lacked in skills, she more than made up for with sloppy and enthusiastic kisses. She had barely left Stacy's side all winter.

"Let's try to find Page, girl," Stacy said to Molly. "She doesn't blend in as well as the wolves do." Stacy set off through the taiga forest, scanning the snowy ground for any signs of fresh tracks. Stacy's wolves—Everest, Basil, Noah, Addison, Tucker, and Wink—were all white with the exception of Addison, whose coat had tinges of brown and rust red. They didn't have to work very hard to hide in the taiga, which had been blanketed in deep snow since they had arrived home right around Christmastime. It was now the end of March, and the snow, which just a few months ago had come up to Stacy's waist, was beginning to thaw.

Ordinarily Stacy would have stuck out like a sore thumb in her usual outfit—a blue-and-white-striped long-sleeve shirt. But today she was wearing her winter coat, which was the same green as the spruce trees and had fake coyote fur trim around the hood. The coat, a gift from the only human who knew Stacy lived in the forest with a pack of wolves, was quickly becoming one of Stacy's favorite possessions. It allowed her to walk around the forest with her wolves and finally feel like she was one of them— especially when she pulled the hood up over her head.

Droplet and Splat, Stacy's two timber wolves, had dark coats mottled with patches of brown, black, and gray. Stacy and the pack hadn't seen much of Droplet and Splat over the last few months. They hung around the cave during the holidays when Addison was baking tasty treats every day, but when Stacy's pack returned to their normal diet of salmon and mushroom stew, Droplet and Splat disappeared into the taiga to hunt. Stacy didn't mind this one bit—she knew that wild wolves needed to hunt to survive and keep the taiga's ecosystem balanced. She guessed they were at least fifty miles away by now, deep in the taiga, and Stacy was just fine with that.

Suddenly, Stacy saw something out of the corner of her eye, a flash of something reddish with a streak of black that disappeared into an old hollow log on the ground: Page's tail. Stacy walked slowly over to the log and leaned down to peer inside.

"Found you!" Stacy exclaimed. Page, startled, whipped around and stared back at Stacy. Molly wagged her tail in excitement and Page followed suit, happy that she had

been found. And in that moment Stacy felt so happy to be in her home in the taiga, with her wolf family and two pet dogs.

"All right, Page," Stacy said with a smile. "You're on our team now. We're the seekers. Let's go find the others, shall we?"

Just as Stacy was talking to Page, a dusting of snow fell in front of her.

"But . . . it's not snowing," Stacy said, perplexed. She looked up into the towering spruce tree above her. "Everest?"

Stacy squinted her eyes and could just make out Everest, her pack's largest wolf, perched in the treetops, the branch swaying under his weight. Stacy chortled at the sight of her largest wolf teetering on a branch that looked like it might break at any moment. *I know you're not afraid of heights, Everest, but be careful up there,* Stacy thought. Everest immediately began to nimbly work his way down the massive spruce. Stacy was still getting used to the fact that Everest could hear her thoughts. She knew Everest was an exceptional wolf—he was their pack's natural leader and the bravest of the group. Stacy even knew he was an unusual-looking wolf, with his pale silver eyes and mammoth size. But the fact that he was a *supernatural* wolf, with the ability to hear her thoughts as plainly as if she was speaking them, was something Stacy had only just discovered recently.

It made sense that Everest had this ability. Every wolf in her pack had developed one. It all began last spring, when Basil was struck by lightning. After she'd recovered from the shock, Basil had been able to run at speeds so fast she could leave a cheetah in her dust. She was also able to summon fire. Noah was the next to develop powers. He could breathe underwater just like the river fish he was so adept at catching. Addison had human-like intelligence and could read and solve math equations, and Tucker was the nurse of the pack. He was skilled at first aid and knew what flowers and plants to apply to wounds to help them heal faster. As for Wink . . . well, Wink was indestructible. He had survived a fall in the mesa that, for any other animal, should have been fatal. *No big deal,* Stacy thought to herself (although she was sure Everest was listening in intently). *I'm living with the craziest pack of wolves in the world.* Of course, Stacy was thrilled to learn the wolves' secrets. She loved her pack more than anything; they were her family, and their abilities were extremely useful to her pack's mission of keeping the creatures of the taiga and its surrounding biomes safe from danger. *But it is strange,* she thought. *Basil got her ability from the lightning strike. But how did my other wolves get their abilities?* It was a question Stacy wasn't even sure the wolves themselves knew the answer to.

Half an hour later, Stacy had found the hiding spots of Basil, Noah, Tucker, and Addison. It turned out Basil hadn't been hiding at all, but rather she'd been following Stacy and quickly darting out of Stacy's sight each time she turned her head. Noah had been the hardest to find—he'd sunk down to the bottom of a pond where he could hold his breath indefinitely. This time of year, the pond was a brilliant dark blue, and Stacy could just make out Noah's white figure underneath the ripples. Stacy had to send Everest down to tell Noah he'd been found. Tucker had been hiding out in an abandoned beaver lodge; Page had sniffed his location out. As for Addison, she had apparently not been interested in the game at all and had used the time to forage for edible mushrooms buried beneath the snow. She'd tucked the mushrooms into the pack on her back, and Stacy suspected they were all going to have stew for dinner that night.

"Let's head home," Stacy said to the others as she turned and began walking in the direction of their cave. "Wink won. He'll figure it out eventually."

As the pack started off for home, Page and Molly

walked directly beside Stacy. Everest and Basil led the way. Addison and Noah brought up the rear of the pack, and Tucker . . . Stacy realized Tucker was no longer with the group. She spun around, her eyes searching everywhere for him. And then she heard a sound that filled her with sudden dread—Tucker's forlorn howl calling out from somewhere in the taiga.

TWO

ALL THE WOLVES, and Page and Molly too, set off in the direction of Tucker's howl. Stacy had no idea which direction Tucker's call had come from, but it was obvious to the wolves and Page, so she was following behind them. It had started to rain, which began to thaw the snow. But Stacy didn't let that slow her. She pumped her arms and ran as fast as she could after the pack, stumbling occasionally through patches of slushy snow.

Stacy caught up to where Page and Molly were and then nudged her way through the pack members to where Tucker was standing. Stacy saw what Tucker had been howling about. He was crouched low to the ground, gently poking an unconscious baby badger with his nose. Stacy let out a small gasp and then walked closer to examine the tiny creature.

The badger cub was gray with black paws and had two black stripes down either side of his face. The middle strip of his head was as white as the melting snow that was all around them. His eyes were shut tight, and the rain beat down on the badger's face, trickling down the white stripe and dripping off his button nose. Stacy knew that badgers were not particularly cuddly animals, but she couldn't help but fall in love.

"Tucker, is it . . . ?" Stacy whispered, but trailed off after she got a good look at the poor creature. The baby badger looked icy and stiff. It needed to be underground with its mother and the rest of its clan. But for whatever reason, it had been out in the cold too long and appeared frozen. Tucker picked up the baby badger by the nape of its neck, lay down, and placed it in the center of his body, curling protectively around the tiny lifeless mammal.

Heat began to emanate from Tucker's body, melting the snow around him and blanketing Stacy and the pack. Stacy couldn't believe what she was feeling. It was almost as if she was standing in front of the cave's fireplace. Tucker had always given the best hugs out of any of her wolves and, if she was being honest, was the wolf she loved snuggling next to the most at night. But could it be that Tucker was able to increase his body heat to whatever temperature he desired?

Stacy thought back to when Basil had been recuperating from her lightning strike. Tucker never left her side. *Had he been keeping her warm then? Performing some other type of healing art that Stacy couldn't see?* Stacy wondered how powerful Tucker's healing abilities really were.

Suddenly, the baby badger wiggled its nose. And then opened its eyes. Stacy couldn't believe what she was seeing. In a matter of seconds, Tucker had been able to raise the baby badger's body temperature and bring it back to life. She threw her arms around him.

"Tucker, you're amazing!" Stacy shouted into his soft

white fur. The baby badger stood up and looked adoringly at Tucker, who in turn gave the badger a slobbery kiss. The badger, full of energy now, scampered past Stacy and the pack and into its burrow just a few feet away, at the base of a large spruce tree.

"Keep warm," Stacy called after it. "It'll be springtime soon!"

Wink was waiting at the cave when Stacy and the pack returned. He spun around a few times in circles and then gave a few excited barks.

"Yes, boy," Stacy said. "You won that game. You're the champ."

Stacy ran to give Wink a quick nuzzle and then stepped into the cave and looked around. The cave had undergone quite a few changes in the months that had passed since they'd returned from the mesa. During the winter, while the wolves were running around during the frequent snowstorms in the taiga, Stacy was stuck inside and so she filled the time working on lots of cave improvement projects. The first thing she'd done was make dog beds for Page and Molly. She whittled down spruce logs into planks and used dovetail joints to join them into boxes with open tops. She'd found a discarded old sleeping bag at the forest's campground that she cut into two pieces and placed inside the wooden frames. But even after she made the dog beds, Page and Molly still usually wound up sleeping with Stacy, snuggled among all the wolves on the cave floor. The effort wasn't wasted, though. It was nice for them to have a place of their own to go to nap during the day. Molly loved to nap and was delighted when Stacy positioned her bed closest to the fireplace. Stacy also crafted wooden bowls for both Page and Molly and carved their names into each. They were smaller than the wolves' wooden bowls, and lighter color as they were carved from birch, but they fit in nicely with the cave's rustic décor.

The next project Stacy completed was a contraption for her chicken, Fluff, so the eggs she laid in her roost at the top of the bookshelves could roll down into a basket without breaking. It made it easy for Addison to collect them whenever she was baking.

Speaking of baskets, Stacy had also gone a little basket crazy. She'd spent a lot of her time indoors crafting baskets out of willows that Noah had brought to her. They weren't perfect baskets, and you could tell which ones Stacy weaved first because they were the most misshapen.

There were baskets all over the cave now: a basket for Fluff's eggs, another for the bread Stacy and Addison baked frequently. A basket with a lid for the few items of clothing Stacy owned. A large basket for all the squash and pumpkins she'd harvested that fed her and the wolves during the winter months. A basket near the fireplace to keep small kindling for Basil to use when she tended to the fire. A basket for the newspapers Addison would fetch for her from the village so that they could do the crossword puzzle together.

Stacy had also made a new broom out of a sturdy birch twig and pine boughs to replace the one she'd worn out sweeping the floor of the cave. And on one particularly cold morning when Stacy was really bored, she'd carved the initials of each member of the pack around the cave's fireplace.

Stacy was proud of the work she'd done around the cave, but she was relieved the snow was thawing. She couldn't wait to get back to what she and her pack did best: animal rescues. And while she loved the fall and winter seasons in the taiga, spring and summer were definitely her favorites. When the weather warmed she could spend as much time as she wanted outdoors with her pack and her pets—exploring new parts of the forest with Everest, going for long walks with Tucker, picking wildflowers and huckleberries with Basil and Addison, playing fetch with Wink, and swimming in the river with Noah.

After the long game of hide-and-seek, Stacy and all the wolves lay down to nap near the cave's hearth. Molly curled up in her bed and looked expectantly at Basil, who stood and walked over to the hearth. Instantly, a fire was roaring, and Molly quickly nodded off. Page took her usual spot in the crook of Stacy's right arm, her head resting gently on Stacy's chest. Addison and Stacy fell asleep quickly, leaning against Tucker, who, she noticed, still felt warm.

Stacy woke up to the smell of mushroom stew. Addison was cooking at the hearth. Only Tucker, Molly, and Page were still sleeping. Wink and Noah were wrestling while Basil set the wolves' bowls out in preparation for the stew. Everest wasn't there—Stacy suspected he was out patrolling the forest. Even though there was no longer a wolf bounty (where hunters were paid to kill wolves) and the taiga had been declared a national forest, Stacy knew that Everest was still worried about humans discovering where Stacy and the pack lived. He kept his guard up, especially as they now had Page and Molly to protect as well. And after the close brush Noah had with Dr. Berg and his research team last fall, Stacy couldn't say that she blamed him for being concerned. If only she could read Everest's thoughts the way he could read hers.

Stacy wondered if she had to be looking at Everest for him to be able to read her thoughts. *Could I think of something now and he would hear me no matter where he was in the taiga?* She looked over at Addison, who was tasting her stew with a pleased expression. Molly was still asleep, but Tucker and Page had woken up and were both groggily looking around the cave. Suddenly, Everest came bounding in and ran over to Stacy and gave her a lick. *Well, that answers that,* she thought. *I guess we're connected no matter where in the taiga the other is.*

Stacy was still thinking about all the ways Everest's telepathy could come in handy as she peered out of the cave's entrance at the setting sun. She reached for her jacket, zipping it up and smoothing out her hair. Stacy had almost forgotten that she had an appointment today and wouldn't be joining the pack for their stew supper.

"Basil, would you mind giving me a ride to the village?" Stacy asked the sleek wolf. Basil stood and trotted over to Stacy, who hopped onto Basil's back. "I told Miriam I'd be there before dark."

THREE

BASIL RAN SWIFTLY through the taiga's trees to the bend in the river where Stacy liked to cross. There were just enough moss-covered stones to make the crossing challenging for Stacy but not impossible. She dismounted Basil and turned to the yellow-eyed wolf.

"I'll be home in a few hours," Stacy said, kissing Basil on the top of her head. "Tell the others not to worry."

Basil began to run and then quickly disappeared into the forest. Stacy turned toward the village and expertly made her way across the river. It was a mile's journey through some cattle fields until she'd reach the little village and the café where Miriam worked.

Miriam Locklear was Stacy's friend—her only human friend. They'd met last summer while Miriam was camping in the taiga. Stacy had also seen her again in the fall, when Stacy snuck into a village council meeting to learn about a potential real estate development that would have demolished the taiga. Luckily, Stacy and her wolves worked to get the taiga designated as a national forest—and in the process, Miriam had discovered Stacy's secret. Stacy had always feared that if a human were to find out there was a girl living in the woods with six wolves, then people would assume she wasn't safe and try to make her leave. But Miriam was different. She trusted Stacy and seemed happy to keep Stacy's secret—and for that Stacy was very grateful. In fact, the coat Stacy wore had been a gift from Miriam at the holidays.

After they saved the taiga, Miriam had moved to the village and started working at the diner, where she invited Stacy for a meal once a week. Stacy delighted in trying new foods—some were things she'd never even heard of before like French fries, tuna salad, grilled cheese, and split-pea soup. Stacy suspected the weekly meal was Miriam's way of making sure Stacy was still healthy and safe, but she didn't mind her concern. Having a friend that she could talk to (who could actually talk back to her) was a treat for Stacy, after all. She welcomed her conversations with Miriam and used them to talk about all sorts of topics, but mostly she wanted to know if Miriam had heard anything about the scientists from the village university who were studying the wolves in the taiga.

Stacy couldn't forget the close call she'd had with them last year when they shot Noah with a tranquilizer dart. Fortunately, the other wolves were able to carry Noah into the cave and hide him from the researchers. Stacy knew the researchers meant no harm and were just trying to collect data to help them understand how the wolves lived in the forest, but she couldn't risk having one of *her* wolves studied. After all, they had special abilities. What if they'd discovered Noah's ability to breathe underwater? They probably would never have released him back into the wild. They would have wanted to run more tests. Stacy and the others might not have ever seen him again.

Stacy skipped through a field of grazing cattle on her way to meet Miriam at the diner. The black-and-white-spotted cows did not startle at her presence but rather kept happily munching away on the grass. Stacy crossed through the field, hopped the gate, and then made her way to the center of town where the village diner was located.

The diner was old and small. But it was cozy and full of delicious smells. Stacy could never decide if she preferred to sit at one of the small wooden booths with red-and-white-checkered tablecloths or on one of the swivel barstools at the front counter, where she could spin around and keep an eye out the window at the village comings and goings.

"Stacy!" Miriam greeted her warmly as Stacy swung open the door to the little diner. Miriam came around the counter and gave Stacy a hug. "Here, I saved a spot at the counter for you," she said, gesturing to the empty stool near the cash register.

Miriam had long black hair, which was tied up in a ponytail, and was wearing a pair of blue jeans and a white short-sleeve blouse. Her skin was a beautiful copper brown. She had an apron on, with a pen and a pad of paper sticking out of the pocket.

Stacy took a seat at the counter near an old man she didn't recognize. She and Miriam had become pretty used to hiding Stacy's identity from nosy villagers. She was usually either Miriam's little cousin visiting from another village or a student on a field trip to Great Taiga National Forest who missed the bus home and was waiting for her parent to come pick her up. Stacy would never say that she *liked* lying about who she was, but it was necessary to protect her wolves, so she didn't feel bad about it one bit.

Half an hour later, Stacy was busy tucking into her tuna melt, French fries, and grapes. She had a tall chocolate milkshake as well. Miriam had been filling Stacy in on the latest village gossip when the conversation suddenly shifted. Miriam hunched over the bar toward Stacy and whispered in a grave tone.

"Dr. Berg from the research team eats here from time to time," she began. "I overheard him say that his team is preparing to collar the wolves in the taiga." Stacy was a little familiar with wolf collaring—she understood that the team would likely use a helicopter to spot the wolves from the sky, shoot them with a tranquilizer dart, and place a collar with GPS around their necks so they would be able to study the wolves' hunting trails. It would be fine for wolves like Droplet and Splat—wolves who had natural instincts and habits. But Stacy knew that none of her six wolves could ever be collared.

"It would be best to lie low for a week or two," Miriam continued in a whisper. "Maybe you could even . . . leave the taiga for a bit?"

The words knocked the air out of Stacy. It had only been last fall that she and the wolves had needed to flee from hunters and leave the taiga. They'd traveled to

the mesa biome—and while Stacy had loved it, she had missed their home cave terribly and she knew the wolves had too. She dreaded the thought of making them leave again.

Stacy thanked Miriam for the information and the meal and was leaving the diner when a small flash of white appeared at her feet and then disappeared into some bushes near the street. Stacy ran over to the bushes to examine it and let out a tiny gasp when she realized what it was.

A cat!

There, tucked into a bush's branches, was a white Siamese cat with a black-and-gray-striped tail and eyes that were so blue Stacy wondered if they were even bluer than Noah's. His nose was small and pink, and several white whiskers protruded from each side of the cat's diminutive snout. This was the first time Stacy had ever seen a cat in real life, and she was struck by how small the cat was. He was skinny too. It looked like it had been weeks since he had had a proper meal.

"Hiding out, hoping for some scraps?" Stacy cooed in the direction of the bushes. "Let me go see if Miriam has anything for you."

Stacy darted back into the diner. A minute later she

emerged with a small red tin of anchovies Miriam had given her.

"I have a feeling you're going to like this," Stacy said, peeling back the top of the anchovy tin and flinging one of them into the bushes, where the cat eagerly gobbled it up. Stacy noticed the cat was blinking his right eye more than the other.

"Oh no, you're injured!" Stacy exclaimed. It occurred to her that this was not somebody's pet, but rather a stray cat in the village who didn't have a home. She tossed the cat another anchovy, and this time he poked his head out from the bushes just far enough for Stacy to pet him. *What happened to you?* Stacy wondered as she stroked the small cat's head. She continued to feed him the anchovies until she'd thrown him the last one. Stacy then put the can down on the ground in front of her. The cat hesitated for a second but then stepped forward toward Stacy and began to lick the juices left in the tiny tin. Stacy sat back and watched the cat, not wanting to scare him off. His eye appeared to have a small amount of blood in it. *Poor thing,* Stacy thought. *I hope he hasn't been in a fight. Or worse . . . abused.* When the cat was finished licking the tin, he lifted his head and looked at Stacy as if to say, *Thank you, I needed that.*

"I've got plenty of food back at my home," Stacy said

softly. She knew the cat couldn't understand her, but even still she felt it best not to mention the six wolves and two dogs that were also at her home. The cat gave her a small meow and began rubbing his face against Stacy's leg. "You're welcome to follow me home, but I've got to get going."

Stacy stood and began to walk away, and to her amazement, the white cat followed her away from the village, through the field, into the taiga, across the river, and home to their cave—purring all the way.

FOUR

NO SOONER HAD Stacy and the cat entered the clearing near the cave than Everest came bounding out to meet her. It was dark, but the full moon shone brightly enough for Stacy to see the concern on Everest's face. He had obviously read Stacy's thoughts and knew that she had brought a cat home with her. Stacy wasn't concerned at all about the cat's safety when it came to the wolves. They didn't hunt or eat any of the small animals that surrounded them in the taiga; Stacy kept them on a strict diet of fish, eggs, pumpkin, and other plants. And of course, they lived with Stacy's chicken,

Fluff, in the cave all the time and were never tempted to eat her even though they'd eaten chicken many times before. Stacy took a minute to consider how the new cat and Fluff would get along. *Well, that should be interesting,* she thought. Molly wasn't a concern— she seemed friendly and not aggressive in the slightest. But Page . . . Stacy (and apparently Everest too) was worried that Page would *not* get along with a cat. Page seemed to have a high prey-instinct, much like Droplet and Splat, and Stacy remembered reading something in a children's book about cats and dogs being natural enemies.

"Everest, I didn't know what to do," Stacy began, but then she remembered she could just *think* what she wanted to say to him. *His eye is hurt and he's starving. He's a homeless stray from the village, and we have such a nice home. Think of him just like any other animal we rescue and rehabilitate. He can stay here in the cave for a few days, at most a week, and get his strength back, and then I can take him back to the village and find him an owner.* Stacy realized she was lying. She wanted to keep the cat for as long as he wanted to stay. Everest shot her a knowing look.

Let's just see how it goes, okay? Stacy thought, scooping

up the cat in her arms and walking through the entrance to the cave. She took a deep breath. "Everyone, there's someone I'd like you all to meet." It came as no surprise to Stacy that the first wolf to come and greet the cat was Tucker. He bounded over and sniffed the cat, who was purring in Stacy's arms. Animals, like the baby badger, instantly felt at ease with Tucker, and the cat was no different. Stacy next walked past Wink, Noah, and Basil, who all raised their heads from their naps to sleepily greet the cat but were, for the most part, uninterested. At first, Stacy was concerned that this meant they didn't like the cat, but then she realized they were all trying not to spook him. Everest also seemed to be keeping his distance. Stacy sensed it wasn't out of not wanting to frighten the cat, but that Everest genuinely thought it a bad decision to try to keep a cat in the cave and so he wasn't getting too attached. The last of the wolves to acknowledge the cat was Addison. She peered down at him, the reading glasses she wore magnifying the cat's tiny features. Stacy could tell that Addison was already thinking through all the ramifications of adding a new family member. Stacy paused to consider them as well. *Where would the cat sleep? What would the cat eat? Would he chase Milo the bat out of the cave each time he came to try to tell the others of an animal rescue?* Despite the reservations the wolf may have had, Addison gave the cat a tiny nod and then went back to tidying up the cave.

Suddenly, Page woke up and realized the cat's presence. She jumped up from where she was lying near the back of the cave and started barking. Molly woke up from her bed near the fire and, sensing Page's excitement, began to howl. Stacy had expected these reactions from her dogs and hugged the tiny cat closer to her. The cat began to tremble.

Suddenly, pandemonium erupted inside the cave. The cat dug his sharp claws into Stacy's shoulders. "Owww!" Stacy gasped and instinctively let go of her hold. The cat catapulted himself off Stacy's shoulders, and jumped onto the shelf where Stacy kept the bowls she used to feed the wolves and dogs, sending them flying. Basil ran to try to catch them and managed to keep a couple from crashing to the ground. Meanwhile, the cat, now even more scared by the sound of the falling bowls, ran to the cave's entrance. "Don't let him leave!" Stacy shouted to whichever of the wolves would listen. "He won't survive a night in the taiga!" Everest knew what Stacy was going to say before she could get the words out and, together with Noah, he blocked the cave opening. Page and Molly were chasing the cat at full speed now. He ricocheted around the cave, weaving his way between baskets and the wolves' legs, searching desperately for a safe place to hide. He scrambled up Stacy's bookcase only to find a hysterical Fluff, who shooed him back down.

"EEEENNNNOUUGHH!" Stacy shouted at the top of her lungs, stepping in front of Page, who skidded to a stop. Molly ran straight into Page and rolled across the floor of the cave before getting to her feet and looking around with a slightly disoriented expression. The cat jumped up on Stacy's desk, knocking over a small bottle of ink.

"Page, it's okay," Stacy said in a soft but firm tone. "This cat is injured, just like all the other animals you help to rescue in the forest." This seemed to finally calm Page, and Molly quickly followed suit and stopped her high-pitched howling. Stacy walked over to the bewildered cat at her desk. He arched his back and stretched and then immediately cowered as Page approached the desk. Page sniffed the cat with an unmistakable look of disdain. It was clear to Stacy that Page accepted having a cat in the cave, but that she was not going to ever be fully on board with the idea. Stacy figured that was okay. Molly came over, curious and wide-eyed. The cat's tail hairs had stood on end and doubled in size during the kerfuffle, but his tail was now smooth and slowly swishing back and forth contentedly.

"I guess you need a name, don't you, fella," Stacy said, turning to the cat. Snowy or Snowball, perhaps. But it was almost spring, and Stacy wasn't sure this cat even liked the snow. She tried to think about what little she knew of the cat's personality, to give him a fitting name. "You're awfully shy but very sweet . . . you're white like snow or . . . milk. I know! What about Milquetoast?" It was one of Stacy's favorite words, usually used to describe someone who was timid or feeble. "We'll work on your shyness, but I think it suits you perfectly!"

Stacy positioned herself on the cat's level and stared into his sparkling blue eyes. The right one was still filled with a pool of blood, and Stacy wondered if she should ask Miriam if she could wash some dishes at the village diner to earn enough money to take the cat to a vet for some medicinal eye drops. No sooner had the thought occurred to her, than Tucker was by her side examining the cat's injury. He pressed his head against the cat's head—Tucker's head was at least five times the size— and when he pulled away, Stacy noticed the cat's eye looked a lot better. He began purring louder than Stacy had heard him purr yet.

"You're healing him, Tuck!" Stacy gasped. She gave Tucker and the cat a big hug. She knew now that bringing Milquetoast home had been the right decision, and that made her so happy. Stacy thought back to when it was just her and the six wolves living in the cave with Fluff. Now she had two dogs, a cat, two timber wolves who visited occasionally, and a bat named Milo. Her pack had expanded so much in such a short period of time, and it filled her with a sense of pride and belonging.

Stacy stroked under the cat's chin with her fingers,

which seemed to give him a little confidence. He puffed up and sat tall and purred. Stacy hadn't realized what a beautiful cat he was. She had been too focused on his injuries and getting him home to her safe, warm cave. The fur on his chest was definitely the whitest, like newly fallen snow. The rest of his body was more cream-colored, except for a few patches of taupe that ran down his back. He definitely didn't seem like a stray, and Stacy wondered what had led to his homelessness.

"All right, it's settled. Milquetoast is part of the family now. That is, if you'll have us, Milquetoast?" She looked at the little cat, who was now curled up and getting a bath from Tucker. "I'll take that as a yes," Stacy said with a smile.

FIVE

STACY WALKED WITH Noah through a particularly muddy patch of the taiga. A week had passed, and snow was melting all over the taiga now, revealing dark brown patches of mud and podzol everywhere Stacy looked. She wished she could splash around in the puddles, but discarded rain boots were something Stacy had never been able to find in the campground and she valued her leather lace-up hiking boots too much. If anything happened to them, she wouldn't be able to go on rescues with her pack. She made sure to keep them in the best condition she could. Noah, on the other hand, jumped in every puddle and patch of mud he could find on their way, rolling around in them until his fur was completely brown instead of his normally brilliant white.

Stacy was accompanying Noah on one of his fishing trips to the river to stock up on salmon for the pack. Noah liked to fish in a particularly deep section of the river where he could catch a lot of salmon that he and Stacy would then take back to the cave. He'd skin and de-bone one or two for Stacy, but the wolves could eat the whole fish, bones and all. Addison used them to make the most delicious salmon stews and fish pies for the pack. Addison also knew how to dry the skins into crispy treats for all the wolves and dogs to enjoy. Stacy was pretty sure Milquetoast would love them too.

In the winter, it was easy to store fish outside in the snow. Other animals in the taiga knew where Stacy and the wolves lived and didn't come near the entrance of the cave. Stacy would dig a little hole in the snow directly outside to store Noah's catches for meals throughout the week. In the summer it was a little more difficult. Stacy kept the fish in the back of the cave, where a little natural spring kept them cool but not frozen. Noah would have to start fishing more regularly in the spring rather than catching lots of fish at one time, since the fish would only stay good for a few days. But Stacy knew it was one of his favorite activities and he wouldn't mind one bit.

Stacy looked up from the ground to see that she and Noah had reached the bank of the river. Noah gracefully dove into the water, immediately cleaning off all the mud, while Stacy sat on a flat rock near the shore. She reached into her satchel and pulled out her journal and a blue ballpoint pen that Miriam had given her. When she told Miriam about the quill and ink bottle she used in the cave, Miriam had whipped the pen from behind her ear and insisted Stacy take it right then. Stacy was grateful for it and dreaded the day it would inevitably run out of ink. Stacy loved writing about her rescue missions in her journal, but now that she had the ballpoint pen, she had begun writing more about her life in the taiga. Today she was planning to write all about Milquetoast. She wanted to keep a record of all the nice memories they'd had in their first week together—like the first time he curled up on Stacy's chest to sleep or how quickly he had become at home in the cave, playing with Molly and keeping Addison company as she baked, angling for scraps.

But something was troubling Stacy and kept her from journaling. She kept thinking about what Miriam had told her about Dr. Berg and his research team. Any day now, they'd be coming into the taiga (or possibly even flying over it in a helicopter!) and attempting to put GPS collars on wolves. Stacy knew it was with the best possible intentions. But she also knew that she couldn't risk one of *her* wolves getting collared. They needed to leave the taiga—and they needed to do it fast. Stacy couldn't bear the thought of leaving Page, Molly, and Milquetoast behind, but she knew that they'd slow the pack down significantly, and they needed to get far away from the taiga as quickly as they could. They'd only need to be gone for a couple weeks most likely, if the information Miriam had given Stacy had been correct, and that made Stacy feel slightly better about leaving her pets alone in the cave.

Stacy looked up to see a family of river otters scampering down the riverbank and plunging into the cold water. Otters were one of her favorite animals aside from wolves and dogs (and now cats). She loved how playful they were. A sudden pang of sadness washed over her again at the thought of leaving this magical place, even if it was only temporarily. She closed her eyes and tried to think of something positive. It would be nice to explore other biomes surrounding the taiga. The last time she left they got to see the mesa biome. It was unlike anything Stacy had ever seen, with stunning red and orange rock formations and flat swaths of sage and cactus that stretched as far as the eye could see. The idea of discovering a new biome was really exciting to Stacy. And of course, she'd be happy to do more animal rescues in whatever biome they found. *How do I go about discovering a new biome? And, if I do find a new biome, what type of animals will we encounter there who need our help?*

Stacy thought about which direction she'd take the wolves. Obviously, they couldn't go west. She didn't know what terrain was past the village, but she knew they wouldn't be able to get around it easily. There were farms and neighborhoods all around the village, so heading west was out of the question. Everest would never allow it. They'd gone south last time and discovered the mesa, but Stacy knew there wasn't much there to eat or see. She longed for adventure. She thought about going east. She knew there was ocean that way. Noah would love to visit the ocean, but it was still too cold this time of year for Stacy to swim. *Wait!* They should go to the north! Stacy had no idea what lay over the tall mountains to the north of the taiga; she had never summited them. It would be challenging, but it was the right time of year to do it, and she knew the wolves would be excited to try. She wouldn't have to talk them into the trek—and Everest had already read her thoughts and knew what Miriam told her. He was resolved that they needed to leave.

North. Stacy thought about it again. It would be cold, but she had the coat from Miriam. The more she thought about it, the more she liked the idea. Of course, it wouldn't be cold for the wolves. Their coats were made to keep them warm in temperatures even lower than the coldest winter nights in the taiga. They were *Arctic* wolves, after all. They must be *from* the north originally, or at least have distant ancestors there! A thought occurred to Stacy that sent shivers down her back. If they went north to where the wolves were from . . . maybe they'd encounter other wolves of their kind—other wolves with special abilities. Maybe they would even be able to track down the secret as to why they had powers!

Stacy peered over the river's edge at Noah, who was swimming gracefully among the romp of river otters. Their bodies were dark brown and sleek, gliding effortlessly through the cold water. The otters expertly dodged and weaved their way around Noah, who seemed thrilled

to be in the company of other mammals who loved the water as much as he did. Stacy watched them for several minutes, none of the animals needing to come up for air. Her decision was made. If there was even a chance Stacy could learn about her wolves' origin in the Arctic, then that was where she wanted to go.

"Noah!" Stacy shouted so the wolf could hear her underwater. "Catch a bunch more . . . we're going on an expedition!"

SIX

STACY TOOK A few steps out of the cave and peered around, looking for any signs of wolf researchers. Instead, she only saw an elk grazing in the distance and an owl perched high up in one of the towering spruce trees that surrounded the cave. The snow was melting everywhere now, sending streams of water trickling down the ridge above the cave.

"Come out, everyone," Stacy said loudly. "The coast is clear."

One by one the wolves and dogs sleepily filed out of the cave to tend to their morning business and sniff around. Only Everest and Basil were alert—everyone else appeared half asleep, particularly Molly, who took an extra-long time to exit the cave.

Stacy had stayed up late making their final preparations to set off on their expedition to the mountains. Everest had read Stacy's thoughts the minute she and Noah had returned from fishing and had agreed that her plan was the best course of action to keep the pack from being discovered by Dr. Berg and his research team.

With the entire pack awake now, everyone walked back into the cave and went to work on their assignments. Noah and Addison were preoccupied with feeding the pack for the trip. Noah filled the wolf saddlebag with all the salmon he'd caught, while Addison was cooking a huge pot of pumpkin soup and individual salmon potpies for everyone to eat before they took off. Wolves don't need to eat every day, and so a hearty meal would sustain them for several days. Stacy liked that plan, given that she had no idea what type of food situation or sleeping arrangements they would find themselves in once they got into the mountains.

Tucker was doing everything he could possibly think of to make sure that Page, Molly, and Milquetoast would be comfortable while the pack was away. Tucker cuddled all three of them, making sure they got extra snuggles to make up for the nights he'd be away. Earlier, he had hidden little treats—dog biscuits that Stacy and Addison had baked, along with dried fish skin—all around the cave for Page, Molly, and Milquetoast to find while the pack was gone. *He's so sweet to do that,* Stacy thought. He even made sure to give Fluff a large pile of seeds and left a cut-up apple near Milo the bat's perch.

Wink was fast asleep by the fire. It was getting almost too warm for fires now, but Basil wanted the cat and dogs to be cozy when they left, so she had gathered lots of wood for them and created the most impressive fire Stacy had ever seen the slender wolf make. It was sure to keep burning for hours, possibly even a full day, before it would die out.

Stacy and Everest were in the back of the cave, examining a map Stacy had of the region. The plan was to head due north, bearing slightly toward the east once they entered the mountain range. Everest had helped Stacy pack her satchel full of the survival equipment she had from their journey to the mesa biome—her binoculars, a utility knife, climbing rope, a compass, Stacy's flint and steel, and some kindling—and a few other odds and ends she'd found in the taiga since then, including a small penlight and a whistle. Stacy also made sure to pack her notebook and ballpoint pen, along with several granola bars Miriam had given her a few weeks prior.

These should sustain me if there's a snowstorm and Basil can't make us a fire to cook with, Stacy thought.

Everyone enjoyed one last meal together as a family, gorging on the potpies and pumpkin soup until they were all full. "We should only be gone for a week or two at most," Stacy said to her pets. She knew they wouldn't fully understand, but she also knew how perceptive Page was. Page was clued into the fact that Stacy and the pack were leaving. And that she wasn't coming, a detail she seemed annoyed with. Stacy had considered bringing Page. The little dog could surely hold her own among the wolves in terms of athleticism and stamina. Page also *loved* the snow. But Stacy knew that Molly was much too delicate to survive a trek through the mountains, and Page would be good company for Molly here in the cave. And although Stacy could not explain this to Page, the little dog seemed to understand and was resigned to her fate.

Stacy retreated to the back of the cave and began to layer what little clothing she had. First, she put on two pairs of socks; next, a pair of long johns underneath her worn blue jeans; and finally, her blue-and-white-striped long-sleeve shirt with a navy blue wool sweater on top and the coat from Miriam on top of that. Hopefully this would keep her warm enough during the days on the expedition. She knew that at night she would be plenty warm, nestled among her wolves with their thick white fur. Speaking of white fur, Milquetoast had come to the back of the cave and was purring and walking in between Stacy's legs, rubbing his head just above her leather boots.

"I'm going to miss you so much," Stacy said, bending down and scooping up the small cat in her arms. "Please don't eat Fluff while I'm gone." The cat looked back at Stacy with a curious expression. Stacy gave him one last squeeze and set him down gently on her desk. She walked over to the cave's entrance and peered outside. The sun was just beginning to rise. If they left now, they'd make it to the mountains by midmorning, probably with enough time to summit their first small peak and make camp before night.

"All right, everyone," she said, addressing the wolves. "Let the expedition begin!"

Stacy and the wolves raced away from the cave, through the taiga to the forest's edge, heading north toward the low mountains in the distance that gave way to higher, more rugged peaks. When her legs got tired, Stacy hopped on Wink's back. It was a good thing he had conserved so much energy by going back to sleep while the other wolves were preparing for the journey.

With Stacy riding on his back, the pack picked up their pace, and they were traversing the low mountains in what seemed like no time at all.

Stacy closed her eyes and let her imagination run wild with the possibilities of what biome she and the pack would discover on the other side of the mountains. This much she knew: this mountain range could stretch for hundreds of miles. On the other side could be a completely different type of biome. She thought of every type of environment she could remember from the books she'd read in the cave. Forest, plains, beach, jungle, savanna . . . to Stacy, they all seemed equally exciting to explore.

Suddenly, Stacy felt herself slipping off Wink. She jerked her head up, opened her eyes, and tightened her grip on the thick fur at the nape of Wink's neck. They were running nearly vertically, climbing up a steep slope. There was snow on the ground now and the pine trees had tall, skinny trunks without any needles. The wolves were expertly weaving in and out of them. Stacy realized they were at an altitude higher than she had ever been before. She took in a deep breath of the thin air and looked back at the vast taiga in the distance—her home. *Good-bye. I'll be back soon,* she thought wistfully. She looked back toward the direction the wolves were running. Stacy couldn't believe it—they were about to summit the peak they were climbing! Everest had wisely chosen the lowest of the peaks for them to ascend.

Suddenly all the wolves stopped running and stood still. They were standing at the top of the mountain, the taiga stretched out behind them, and in front of them was white as far as Stacy's eyes could see. She realized at once what type of biome she and the pack had discovered.

Tundra.

SEVEN

STACY COULDN'T BELIEVE what she was seeing. All the years she'd lived in the taiga and stared up at the very mountain range that she and the wolves were now currently standing atop . . . a giant tundra biome had been beyond the mountains. *Is this where my wolves are from?*

Stacy looked at Everest, Addison, Noah, Tucker, Basil, and Wink. Their expressions were like her own—surprise and shock mixed with curiosity and wonder. The seven of them stared out over the frozen terrain. It was virtually treeless; it was too cold for trees to survive.

The tundra was untouched and pristine—just waiting to be explored.

Maybe Everest read Stacy's thoughts or maybe they were all thinking the exact same thing. Either way, without any words being exchanged, Stacy and the wolves began to make their way down the mountain toward the tundra. A small snowshoe hare scampered away from them as they descended the craggy cliffside to the foot of the mountains.

"Is everyone okay?" Stacy asked once they were all on level ground. She looked at the wolves and then to the flat snowfield that lay in front of them. Basil was pacing back and forth, nervously twitching. Wink's head was moving around rapidly, taking in all the sights. Tucker was stretching. Addison was adjusting Tucker's pack for him. Noah's tail was wagging wildly. And Everest was taking deep breaths, as if he couldn't get enough of the tundra air. *What's going on?* Suddenly, a thought occurred to Stacy. *They want to run.* Stacy looked at her wolves, lined up at the tundra's edge. *Their instincts must be kicking in. They want to run!* Stacy jumped on top of Basil and gave the okay. With the mountains now directly behind them, Stacy and the pack set off across the vast tundra. She couldn't believe how expansive the biome was. As she bobbed up and down on Basil's back,

Stacy marveled at how the white ice kissed the gray sky. The horizon stretched out for what Stacy imagined must be a hundred miles.

My wolves seem to love it here, Stacy thought. *But they also act like they've never been here before. Or maybe they just haven't been here in a long time. Either way, they all seem very happy to be on the tundra.*

Everest let out a loud bark of agreement. The pack was now running faster than Stacy had ever seen them run. Even though it was white and snow-covered, something about the tundra reminded Stacy of the mesa. It was open. There were no trees to dodge, rocks to jump over, or bushes to go around—everything was flat and wide open. The wolves were charting a course north, and Stacy was happy that she didn't have to worry about making sure they knew how to find their way home. Everest was an expert navigator and always seemed to know the way back to the taiga regardless of where they were.

The pack ran for an hour, stopping occasionally for short water breaks. Tucker would use his body heat to melt a small patch of ground to a puddle of crystal-clear ice water for everyone to drink from. Stacy filled her canteen and sipped the cool water, impressed by the use of Tucker's ability. The sun was directly overhead at this point, so it wasn't too cold for Stacy, even when she was riding on Basil's back. Stacy figured they must be fifty miles north of where the tundra began by now, and they had yet to see any other signs of life aside from the snowshoe hares and one ornery marmot that wanted nothing to do with them.

Stacy glanced up and noticed they were approaching a bright blue pond. *This could be a nice place to camp,* Stacy thought to herself, when she saw something out of the corner of her eye. *Could it be?* Everest, hearing Stacy's thoughts, quickly veered to the right.

"Polar bear cub!" Stacy shouted to the rest of her pack, who immediately changed direction and followed Everest. The cub was standing on the edge of the pond, peering down into the sparkling water. *If it's orphaned, we will have to take it in,* Stacy thought. Her mind started to race as Basil carried her the couple hundred feet toward where the cub was standing. *What do polar bear cubs eat? Could the cub keep up with me and the pack on the rest of our expedition? Would we bring it home to the taiga? Would it be okay in the summer months when the taiga was slightly warmer than the tundra? What would happen when the cub grew up? How would it fit in the cave with the others? Would it want to eat Page and Molly?*

All these thoughts flew through Stacy's mind in the

thirty seconds it took for them to reach the cub. Now they were just a few dozen steps from where it was standing at the water's edge. Stacy looked closer—the cub couldn't have been more than a few months old. Its fur was fluffy and white, and it had the most adorable tiny ears and black button nose. Its paws were much too big for it, but it would certainly grow a lot over the next year. Stacy hopped off Basil and reached into the satchel on Tucker's back, pulling out one of the large salmon Noah had caught before their trip. Holding the salmon in her outstretched arms, she began to slowly walk toward the polar bear cub. The cub looked up at her inquisitively and took a step closer to the water. The wolves stayed back, except for Wink, who was just as curious as Stacy.

"Hey, little one," Stacy said in a soft tone. "Where's your momma?" The cub made no move toward them, but instead inched even closer to the pond. Suddenly, a massive adult polar bear leapt out of the water and onto the snow, protectively standing over its cub. Water dripped from every inch of its muscular body. Its huge yellow teeth held a dead fish in its mouth, which it dropped at Stacy's feet so that it could let out a deafening roar. The noise blew Stacy's hair back and sent a shiver down her spine. This moment might have been the most scared she'd ever been in her entire life. Stacy looked at

Wink, who was equally terrified, and then back up at the mighty bear, who looked like it was deciding whether to attack Stacy or Wink first.

All the other wolves—Everest, Tucker, Basil, Addison, and Noah—quickly circled themselves around Stacy and Wink, growling and baring their teeth. This seemed to confuse the bear. It let out another roar, but this one sounded almost like pleading. It occurred to Stacy that any other wolf pack might have surrounded a polar bear and a cub and distracted the mother bear long enough (nipping at her and biting her) for the other members of the pack to kill her cub and drag it away. The grim thought made Stacy sad. How could she convey to the polar bear that they instead had been interested in helping her cub?

"Back away from the cub," Stacy said loudly but calmly. "That's her only concern." Stacy and the wolves retreated quickly to a safe distance away from the bear and her cub. It was only then that Stacy noticed the bear was very skinny. Stacy grabbed the rest of Noah's salmon from Tucker's pack and laid them on the ground. "You can catch more, boy," she said to Noah. "She needs them for her cub." Noah understood and gave Stacy a nod. Stacy looked back at the polar bear, who was busy looking her cub over for injuries. *It must have been so scary for her to be underwater searching desperately for a meal for her and her cub and then to hear a pack of wolves and a human up at the surface. We must have given her such a fright.* Stacy looked over at Everest, who was busy surveying the tundra for signs of any other polar bears. He gave Stacy a nod that seemed to say that they should get going and move farther away from the polar bear and her cub. Stacy couldn't agree more. It had been a thrill to see a polar bear up close in the wild, but that had been a little *too* close for Stacy's liking.

Stacy and the others set off to the north again, walking this time, with Everest leading the way. Stacy thought about the fact that she had left her bow and arrow back at the taiga. There was no way she would ever in a million years have drawn her bow on that mother bear and her cub. She'd rather die than do that. But it did occur to her how vulnerable she would be on the tundra if she was somehow separated from her wolves. Of course, there was no way Everest would ever let that happen—of that Stacy was certain.

They walked leisurely for a few hours, enjoying the tundra's monochromatic scenery until the sunset turned the sky the most beautiful shades of lavender, light blue, and pastel pink that Stacy had ever seen. While the wolves frolicked in the evening light, Stacy sat down on a boulder and sketched the sunset—lamenting that she only had a blue pen instead of paints or colored pencils.

It was only when the last glimmer of sunlight had disappeared from the horizon and the wind began to blow and howl across the frozen biome that Stacy and the wolves realized they had no shelter, no food, and no plans for getting through the night. . . .

EIGHT

"I'M SORRY!"

Stacy felt herself panicking. She wasn't sure how the night had crept up on her, but it was dark now and she hadn't a clue what she and her pack would do now that the temperature had dropped. Even though her wolves took care of her in almost every regard she could think of, Stacy still felt responsible for them and felt terrible for not making a better plan for this trip. She was about to cry, when Basil came over and lit Stacy a torch so she could see what the wolves were doing around her.

Tucker was walking in a circle around them, his body heat thawing the snow to reveal patches of mossy earth that Wink was pawing at and loosening to create a soft spot for everyone to sleep. Everest and Noah were creating a short ice wall out of snow to shelter them from the wind. And Addison had laid out a small supper for Stacy consisting of pumpkin bread, two hard-boiled eggs, and some dried apple slices. While Stacy ate, Addison wandered about thirty paces past where Everest and Noah were building. She was looking at something on the ground where Wink had set aside some sticks he found while clearing the ground, which he used to start a small, glowing fire.

"You guys are amazing," Stacy said in a hushed tone as she popped an apple slice into her mouth. "I guess I had nothing to worry about."

Stacy finished her meal, and she and all the wolves curled up around each other for the night. Stacy hadn't slept outside under the stars since the night in the mesa last fall. Of course, then it had been warm, while tonight she needed all the wolves around her keeping her from freezing on the tundra.

Wink nosed Stacy awake before the sun was up. Stacy sat up and groggily looked around. She was instantly cold and buttoned her coat up all the way and cinched the hood around her face.

"What's going on?" she asked Wink. "Is everything

okay?" Stacy looked around to see the wolves had cleaned up all traces of their camp and were ready to leave. She slowly got to her feet. Basil came over and knelt beside her, a signal for Stacy to climb on her back. Stacy wasn't sure why the wolves were so anxious to leave. As far as she knew, they had no plans or destination in mind. There were no animals she knew of that needed rescuing. But she was happy to oblige and sleep on Basil's back as they traveled.

As they began to cross the tundra, Stacy noticed that Addison was in the lead now and that she kept looking toward the sky. Every few minutes Addison would look to the sky and then slightly alter her direction, with the rest of the wolves following behind her. Stacy tilted her head up, looking for a bird or a bat . . . something that Addison was following. But she only saw the stars, barely visible now against the pale blue-gray light of the morning. Suddenly it dawned on Stacy—Addison was using the stars to navigate! *But where is she leading us? Is Addison taking us somewhere?*

Dawn came, and it was spectacular. Yellow light spilled over the icy horizon like a tipped-over can of paint. Stacy noticed patches of the ground far in the distance that were glinting more than others in the sun. *Water!* The tundra broke off into miles and miles of ice floes that extended to the north and the east.

"Up ahead," Stacy yelled. "Noah can fish!" The pack rerouted toward the ice floes and reached them after a few minutes. Addison, Everest, Tucker, Basil, and Wink stopped to drink while Noah happily dove into the arctic waters. He tossed a large fish up onto one of the floes and dove back under the water. The fish flapped around wildly for a few seconds on the ice before lying still. Stacy knew that Noah would catch exactly thirteen fish: two for each of the wolves and one more that he would filet for her and cook over one of Basil's fires.

"Noah's going to be awhile," Stacy said, turning to the others. "Basil, why don't you and Tucker go scout ahead and see which direction we should take next?" The wolves nodded in agreement and set off to the west. Wink had hopped between ice floes over to where Noah was fishing and was already eating his two fish. *Typical Wink,* Stacy thought. *Are you hungry, Everest?* Stacy turned to see Everest lying on the ground, asleep. Stacy realized he must have stayed awake most of the night, keeping guard. He was exhausted, but something about his face looked content too—happy to be in the tundra with Stacy and his wolf family. Stacy decided they should let him sleep as long as he wanted.

"Addi, maybe we should . . . ," Stacy started, but then

suddenly realized that Addison was not next to her. She looked around. "Addison?"

Stacy saw the wolf way in the distance. It helped that Addison's coat was not solid white like the others' but had light brown in it. Addison was studying a part of the ice a few hundred feet away from where Stacy was standing. *Did she find a small animal that needs help?* Stacy walked over to her, but as she got closer, she saw that there was no animal. Instead, Addison was staring at a series of grooves in the ice in front of her. A peculiar feeling washed over Stacy. The grooves were strange— they weren't random marks in the ice that could have been done by erosion. They were linear and distinctly shaped. *Is it a word?*

"Addi, can you read this?" Stacy asked, looking at the studious wolf. Addison nodded slowly, almost as if Addison herself could not believe that she knew how to read it. Stacy was incredulous. *What language is it? How does Addison know it? Does this have something to do with Addison using the stars to navigate?* Stacy took out her journal and her pen from her satchel and sketched the symbols. She wanted to remember them.

Stacy was just finishing sketching the last symbol, sort of a V shape, when Wink let out an ear-piercing howl back at the ice floes.

"Wink!" Stacy yelled, packing up her journal and racing back toward him with Addison. Everest was awake and standing at the edge of the ice, barking at . . . something. Stacy could not reconcile what she was seeing. Surrounding Wink were what looked to be at least a dozen long spikes, each ten or twelve feet in length. And they were moving. Wink had obviously been poked by one of the sharp-looking spikes. Stacy pumped her arms, running as fast as she could toward the commotion. As she approached the spot where Everest was standing, she realized the spikes were attached to animals bobbing up and down in the water. Narwhals! Stacy had read about them in *Moby Dick* by Herman Melville, a classic she and Addison had slogged through over the winter. Melville had called the narwhal a Tusked Whale, or a Unicorn Whale, with a large "ice-piercer" protruding from its jaw. When Stacy had read about them, she was certain that she would never see one in real life. She was overwhelmed at the sight of an entire pod of narwhals making their way through the ice floes. Some had leopard-like spots, just as Melville had described, while others were more solid gray. And Stacy noticed some that didn't have tusks at all.

Suddenly, Noah popped up from underwater in the middle of the narwhal pod, looking utterly perplexed. He swam to a nearby sheet of ice and deposited what looked to be the last of the fish he needed to catch in a heaping pile next to Wink, who was sheepishly nursing his narwhal poke.

"It's okay, guys," Stacy shouted to Everest, Noah, and Wink. "They aren't aggressive at all. And Wink, aren't you supposed to be indestructible anyway?" Stacy couldn't help but tease the youngest wolf in the pack. She wished more than anything that she still had the camera she'd borrowed from Miriam's friend last year so that she could take a picture of the majestic creatures. Stacy sat near the edge of the ice floes and watched the narwhals until they had all made their way through the small passages farther inland.

Stacy stood up and turned to see Everest, Addison, Tucker, and Wink all napping in a big dog pile. Basil and Tucker were still out scouting. Just then, she noticed a small, spotted narwhal that was lingering nearby in the floes.

"Your friends all went that way," she called, walking

over to see how close she could get to the narwhal. Stacy wondered why he hadn't kept up with his pod. Suddenly she realized the gravity of the narwhal's situation. His tusk was stuck in the ice. *He was trapped.*

"Help!" she called to the others. "Animal rescue!"

NINE

STACY WAS FIRST to reach the young narwhal. She reached down over the edge of the ice and touched his spotted back, which was just under the surface of the water. Stacy assumed he was a young whale because his tusk, which was actually just a very large, overgrown tooth, was only about four feet long. And it was currently jammed into a thick slab of ice. The whale must have been swimming too fast in this section of the ice floes and rammed into the ice—or maybe he had been trying to break up some of the ice to make more room for his pod members and misjudged how thick this part of the ice was—and now he couldn't wriggle himself free.

He was fully submerged underwater, his blowhole just inches from the air, which meant he was holding his breath. Stacy reckoned narwhals could hold their breath for a long time (much longer than a polar bear), but she also knew that this was a mammal and it needed oxygen to live. She guessed he could stay underwater for twenty to twenty-five minutes at most. And she had no idea when he had become stuck . . . which meant that time was running out for this narwhal. Stacy shuddered to think what could happen if they didn't help free it in time. She peered down into the water and saw the panic in the narwhal's eyes.

"Everest!" Stacy called to her strongest wolf. "Come help me try to push him free." Everest was by Stacy's side in an instant. Stacy clasped her hands around the base of the narwhal's tusk, half of which was in the ice. Everest carefully took the section of tusk closest to the ice in his mouth, and they began trying to push the narwhal backward. It was no use. Noah jumped in the water and tried to push the narwhal away from the ice from underneath. Addison paced back and forth near Stacy and Everest—studying the situation to work out the best angles for Stacy and the others to direct their efforts. Meanwhile,

Wink began chipping away at the ice with his jaw.

"Careful, Wink!" Stacy cautioned. "You'll chip a tooth or someth . . ." Stacy's voice trailed off, remembering that this particular wolf of hers actually seemed incapable of breaking a bone or, in this instance, a tooth.

Stacy and the wolves worked hard for the next few minutes, to no avail. Stacy could tell the narwhal, who she had already nicknamed Norman, was losing hope. He had been attempting to swim backward, away from the ice, but now he was exhausted and seemed almost resigned to his fate. *If only we could melt the ice, just a little,* Stacy thought. No sooner had the thought entered her mind than Everest relinquished his grip on Norman's tusk, turned to the west, and let out a loud, bellowing howl. *Of course! Tucker! Tucker could melt the ice! But he could be miles away, what if he doesn't make it in time?*

It was Basil that Stacy saw first. She was running toward them at full speed. She reached them seconds after Stacy saw her in the distance. Everest briefed Basil on the situation and what they needed Tucker to do, and then Basil ran back the way she came to relay the information to Tucker, so there would be no time wasted explaining the narwhal's predicament when he reached them.

Minutes passed. Precious time. Stacy was beside

herself imagining how hopeless Norman must be feeling now that they'd paused their rescue efforts to wait for Tucker.

"It's going to be okay," she said, trying to soothe the narwhal. But she wasn't even sure he could hear her underwater, let alone understand.

Stacy looked up to see Tucker and Basil charging toward them. Tucker had a determined look on his face and . . . almost looked like he was . . . glowing. Stacy realized he was raising his body temperature quickly so he would be very hot once he got to them. Everyone assumed their positions around Norman in anticipation of Tucker's arrival. Tucker reached them and lay down on the ice where Norman's tusk was trapped several feet below. The ice began melting.

"Okay, everyone!" Stacy shouted. "PUSH!" Everest and Stacy pushed on the tusk while Noah pushed on Norman's body from underneath the ice shelf. Addison came over and adjusted Stacy's arm, showing her which angle to push in, which Stacy did with everything she had. Beads of sweat began to accumulate on Stacy's forehead from how hard she was pushing and from standing next to a burning-hot Tucker.

Suddenly, Norman was free! He glided about five feet back in the water, away from the ice, but remained motionless. *Come on, Norman,* Stacy thought, as Noah swam up beside him and nuzzled the whale. Norman began to stir and then quickly surfaced above the water, taking in oxygen through his blowhole. Stacy and the others breathed huge sighs of relief. Stacy threw her arms around Tucker. Addison, Everest, Wink, and Basil piled on top of them, overcome with happiness that they'd been able to save the narwhal. Everyone stood and watched Noah and Norman playing in the water. Stacy wondered how—

K-K-K-K-K-K-K-K-K-R-R-R-R-A-A-A-A-A-A-A-C-C-C-K-K-K-K-K

A huge crack appeared in the ice where the narwhal had been stuck. The tundra began splitting in two. Sheets of ice crashed down into the icy waters, splashing violently.

And the crack was headed straight toward where Stacy and the pack were standing.

TEN

"RRRRUUUUNNNN!!!" STACY SHOUTED as loud as she could so her voice would be heard over the deafening noise of the ice shelf breaking off and crashing into the water. Stacy turned away from Noah, who was treading water next to Norman. Stacy and the rest of the pack began to race across the tundra away from the growing crevice. All the other wolves were ahead of Stacy. Basil was the farthest away, followed by Everest, Addison, Tucker, and Wink. Stacy looked back to see that the crack was catching up to her—dozens of little splinters in the ice were visible beneath her feet. Behind her, the splinters were turning to fissures and then to large, craggy fractures that broke off and fell at least twenty feet into the arctic waters.

Oh no. Stacy realized she was not going to be able to outrun the crack. *If I fall into the water, maybe Noah will be able to help me to the surface. And then maybe Tucker will be able to get my body temperature back above freezing. That is . . . if I survive the fall.* Stacy knew she couldn't think like that. She pumped her arms and tried to run faster. But it was no use. The ground underneath her began to tremble, causing Stacy to stumble slightly as she tried in vain to accelerate.

This is it for me, Stacy thought. *I wish I could say good-bye to Page, Molly, and Milquetoast.*

Suddenly Everest let out a loud series of barks. Basil, hearing and understanding the meaning, immediately reversed course, running back to save Stacy. Stacy leapt onto Basil's back just as a large piece of ice broke from under her. Basil nimbly propelled them up onto the tundra again and quickly raced past Wink and the others back to the front of the pack. Stacy gripped Basil's fur tightly and turned back to look at the others. Everest was close behind. Addison and Tucker were in the middle, and Wink was bringing up the rear. Stacy knew Wink

could survive falling into the water unscathed, but she also knew that he could not hold his breath indefinitely like Noah. She closed her eyes. *Please let my wolves run as swiftly as they can. Please let my wolves be safe.*

Stacy felt Basil veer to the left. The others followed in hopes of clearing the destruction of the ice shelf breaking off behind them. It worked—the wolves put good distance between themselves and the ice rubble, which was still breaking off and settling—creating large, frothy swells in the water.

Stacy breathed a massive sigh. She didn't realize she had been holding her breath. Basil stopped running and turned around as the other wolves caught up to her.

"Is Noah okay?" Stacy asked the entire group, hoping that one of them knew the answer. Everest nodded, pointing with his nose northeast, where the water was much calmer. Noah and Norman were there, bobbing up and down in the water. Stacy and the group ran over to them. Now that the danger of the ice shelf breaking apart was over, Stacy and her wolves had a surge of adrenaline rush over them.

"That was so cool!" Stacy exclaimed, running up to the edge of the ice and patting Noah on the head. "Mother Nature sure is powerful, huh?" She looked at

Norman and wondered if narwhals had the same kind of feelings humans did.

"Don't worry, fella," she said to Norman. "You didn't cause that with your tusk. Part of the ice breaking off like that and forming a giant iceberg is something that would have been years in the making . . . maybe even decades." The narwhal had no change in facial expression. Stacy wasn't surprised, but she always liked to assume an animal could understand her just like her wolves could, especially an animal as magical-looking as a narwhal. *Why did the ice shelf break off like that though,* she wondered. *Was it too warm? Will this disrupt the lives of the animals who live in this remote part of the world?* Stacy thought about the narwhal pod, the polar bear and her cub, and all the snowshoe hares they'd seen. It made her sad thinking about whether some of them might have had homes in the path of the destruction.

"Listen, Norman," Stacy said. "I know you can't understand me, but I hope you keep swimming north and can find your pod. And I hope we see you again sometime."

Stacy was positive Norman could not understand, but the narwhal gave her and the pack a sort of bow in the water and swam away. Stacy and the wolves watched as he glided gracefully under the water.

"Listen, guys, I know we've rescued a lot of animals," Stacy said with her arms around Everest and a very soggy Noah. "But that *had* to have been our coolest rescue yet."

ELEVEN

STACY AND EVEREST walked behind the other pack members. Several hours had passed and Stacy had been thinking a lot about the markings in the ice that she had seen Addison reading.

"Okay, so these . . . *runes* . . . if that's the right word for them," Stacy whispered before remembering she didn't need to speak for Everest to hear her. *You knew she was reading them?* Everest nodded. *And you can read them too?* Everest shook his head no. Stacy considered this for a moment. *Addison knows a language that Everest doesn't. But how?* Everest shook his head at that thought as well. *And does she know where they're leading us?* Everest shook his head. Another no. Stacy thumbed through her journal as they walked and found the page where she had scrawled the runes. She looked at the symbols carefully. They were unlike anything she had seen in any of the books back home on her bookshelf in the cave. Of that she was certain. And *that* meant that Addison had either instantly been able to read them or that she had learned how to read them before Stacy had come to live with her in the taiga. Both possibilities were equally puzzling to Stacy. But whichever it was, Stacy understood that Addison trusted the runes for some reason. And that's why she was leading Stacy and the others in the direction they were telling her to go. *But where is that? And what will we find when we get there?*

Stacy noticed the others had stopped walking. She and Everest caught up to where they were standing, each of Stacy's wolves looking out across the tundra. Stacy followed their gaze and let out a small gasp. In the distance was a large patch of brown . . . *Is it an island?* Stacy looked harder and rubbed her eyes. *Can I really be seeing what I think I'm seeing?* The large brown mass wasn't an island. It was . . . *reindeer.* There must be hundreds, congregated in a giant herd on the tundra. She looked back at her wolves. Everest's face bore a troubled expression, as if he was already working something out in his head.

Basil looked tense. Wink looked excited. Stacy felt the same. She had never seen reindeer before and guessed Wink hadn't either.

"There are so many," Stacy said in wonder. Everest nodded seriously and Stacy suddenly understood the reason for his concern. These reindeer were resting— most likely stopping to eat and sleep as part of a long herd migration. If any of them saw a pack of wolves, the reindeer would panic, and chaos would erupt on the tundra. The thought had occurred to Stacy that they could encounter other Arctic wolves on their expedition, but meeting a herd of reindeer on the way hadn't crossed her mind.

"We've got to go around them," Stacy decided. Addison nodded in agreement. Stacy turned to look at Everest, but he wasn't there. She looked around at the other wolves—Tucker, Basil, Addison, Wink, Noah . . . Everest had been with them seconds before. *Where did he go?* Stacy surveyed the tundra all around them. It was so flat. She should be able to still see Everest even if he had, for some reason, left the pack to walk somewhere else. She turned back around and realized she was staring directly at Everest, who was looking down at himself with a shocked look.

"Everest, you're back!" Stacy exclaimed. "Where did

you go? It was like you disappeared."

Everest looked at Stacy, his silver eyes uneasy. He motioned for Stacy to look down at his paws. She followed his gaze and stared at his snowy white paws on the tundra snow. Suddenly, and yet somehow slowly, Everest's fur started to shift around and he began to blend in with the tundra. First his paws, then his legs and underbelly, then his chest and head, and finally, his tail. Stacy's jaw dropped as she stared at the icy ground where Everest had been standing. Up close, Stacy could still make out the outline of the large wolf. And his piercing silver eyes were still visible. But the rest of him was perfectly camouflaged with the snow—almost like a chameleon taking on the color of whatever rock it was lying on.

"You . . . you *did* disappear," Stacy gulped. Slowly, Everest came back into focus. "Have . . . have you ever done that before?" Everest moved his head back and forth very slowly. Stacy got the distinct impression that not only had Everest never camouflaged himself before, but he also didn't know he could.

The other wolves stared at their alpha in disbelief. Everest began to walk slowly in a circle around them and suddenly they all began to take on the extreme camouflage. Stacy stared in wonder at the six wagging tails that remained visible until they, too, blended in with the surroundings and the only traces left of Stacy's wolves were their different-colored eyes and the fish-filled pack Tucker was wearing, which looked as if it was hanging in midair.

Stacy stretched out her hands. She felt something soft—*so soft*—Tucker. And then another wolf passed by her. This one was taller . . . Everest. And then a slobbery wet tongue touched her hands. Wink. Stacy spun around in circles, in disbelief that all her wolves were now practically invisible around her.

"Everest, I don't know how you're doing this," Stacy whispered. "But this is *so* cool. Is the plan to walk *through* the reindeer?" Everest's head reappeared and he nodded yes to Stacy before becoming camouflaged again.

Stacy considered Everest's plan. She was pretty sure reindeer would still be able to smell the wolves, but without seeing any wolves around . . . maybe Everest's idea would work after all. "All right," Stacy said softly. "Let's go then, but please do not bump into any of them and cause a stampede around me. I'm looking at you, Wink. Except . . . well, I'm not actually since you're invisible. But you know what I mean." Stacy felt Wink's wet tongue kiss her cheek.

They set off across the tundra in the direction of the reindeer, with six sets of pawprints appearing in the snow alongside Stacy's. She was exhilarated by Everest's newfound ability, but panic bubbled up inside her as she approached the first reindeer on the edge of the herd.

Can Everest keep all the wolves camouflaged for the entire length of time it will take to walk through the herd? Will the effect wear off after a while? What if the reindeer smell the wolves? Will they get startled and run?

The reindeer had impossibly large hooves and soft-looking silver-brown fur. Their antlers were tall and narrow. One reindeer looked up at Stacy but didn't seem to mind her being there. Stacy gulped and slowly walked by, carefully selecting a route that would get her through the herd quickly and quietly. She counted the reindeer as she passed by them. She lost count around seventy-two, though. Some of them did seem startled at the sight of a human girl walking toward them, but their reactions were nowhere near as worried as they would have been had they looked up to see six large Arctic wolves coming their way.

It took Stacy almost ten minutes to walk through the entire herd. When she reached the final few reindeer, she started to run on the open tundra. She got a good distance away from them and turned to see the wolves begin to reappear, one by one.

"We did it!" Stacy exclaimed, throwing her arms

around a still reappearing Everest. A euphoric sense of relief washed over Stacy and she was sure the wolves felt the same way. "That could have been so bad. Everest, you saved the day with your new power."

Everest was beaming with pride and Stacy felt so happy for the alpha wolf. Not that his ability to hear Stacy's thoughts hadn't been extremely useful, but it wasn't the . . . *coolest* power of the pack. Invisibility, on the other hand, was right up there with Basil's speed. Basil also had the power to light fires. Up until now, Basil and Tucker (who could heal wounds *and* increase his body temperature) had been the only ones of Stacy's wolves who had multiple abilities. It made sense though that the pack's leader would also have multiple powers. *Will Addison, Wink, and Noah get new powers too? What caused Everest to suddenly have a new ability?*

Stacy was tired from hours of walking and the suspense of the trek through the reindeer herd, so she climbed on Wink's back so the pack could run as Addison recharted a course for them to the northwest. Addison seemed so confident in the direction she wanted the pack to run. Stacy wondered what the runes said and if she'd ever be able to read them like Addison.

After hours of running, the sun disappeared, and the pack stopped and made camp for the night. Stacy could barely keep her eyes open as she tried to finish the fish filet Addison cooked her. Not only was she exhausted, but she was cold. Freezing, in fact. The air was much colder on the tundra this far north, as the sun wasn't up for as long during the day. Stacy fell asleep before she could wish her wolves a goodnight, but they made sure to position her closest to Tucker, who raised his temperature slightly to keep Stacy warm all night long.

It wasn't until the dim morning light came and Stacy awoke and saw the ominous shapes looming in the distance that she realized they had been sleeping on the edge of an entirely new and mysterious biome: ice spikes.

TWELVE

STACY SURVEYED THE ice spikes in the distance as she sipped on the piping-hot cup of huckleberry tea Addison had prepared for her. *Does she want to go through them, Everest?* The large wolf nodded, and Stacy noted a slight sense of trepidation in his movements.

The ice spikes looked . . . dangerous. They were impossibly large, craggy ice crystals that extended thirty or forty feet into the sky and looked as if they could break off and fall on them at any moment. There was also no way to see what dangers might await them once they entered the icy biome. It wasn't like the open ice plains of the tundra where they had room to run to safety if there was another crack in the ice or if they stumbled into the den of a polar bear. They'd essentially be trapped in an ice maze. Stacy trusted Addison, but she would be lying to herself if she said she wasn't worried.

"I'm just not sure it's a good idea, Addi," Stacy said as Addison walked up and sat in front of her. Tucker, meanwhile, came up behind Stacy to comfort her. He rested his nose on Stacy's shoulder and Stacy reached up to pet him. Tucker could always sense if she was upset or worried about something. And he could always make her feel better.

"Where are we going anyway?" Stacy continued. "And why are we going there? You know something that you aren't telling me, but I know it's not your fault you can't explain it." Stacy desperately wished there was a way that Addison could communicate with her and tell her why she was leading them so far north. Stacy was beginning to wonder if it would have been better to set up camp somewhere for the duration of their time on the tundra instead of continuously running farther north—farther away from the taiga . . . and farther away from Page, Molly, and Milquetoast. *Maybe that's what is really bothering me? Maybe I'm homesick for the cave and my pets?*

And it's upsetting that we keep traveling even farther away from them.

Addison took a long stick from the fire Basil was tending to and used the hot end to draw in the snow. She spent several minutes carving an intricate series of symbols, only a few of which Stacy recognized.

Stacy, Everest, Basil, Noah, Wink, and Tucker all gathered around the runes Addison had drawn into the snow. Stacy looked at them for a moment and then turned to survey the wolves' expressions. Everest was studying them intently, desperately wanting to understand. Basil's eyes darted around wildly, but it didn't look to Stacy like she could read them either. Tucker and Noah looked equally perplexed. Wink appeared downright baffled.

"Addi, we can't read this," Stacy said softly, not wanting to hurt Addison's feelings. "I wish we could, but only you can."

Addison looked at Stacy earnestly and Stacy put her

arms around her. "If it's really important to you that we keep going, we will," Stacy said. "We trust you, Addi." Addison nodded.

"Okay, everyone," Stacy said, turning to the rest of the wolves. "We're going into the ice spikes. Everest and Addison will lead. Tucker, you take the rear so you can see if anyone needs help. Wink and Noah, you guys can walk on either side of me. And Basil, I'd prefer if you didn't scout up ahead. We don't know what kind of danger there will be, and I think it's best that we don't get separated. If we stick together, we can face any obstacles we encounter head on . . . as a pack."

Basil and the other wolves all nodded and took their places around Stacy as she started off in the direction of the ice spikes. Stacy looked up as they approached the first spire, in awe of the towering blueish obelisk. She scanned the horizon and counted sixteen other tall crystals surrounding them. And that was just what she could see right now. Soon, they were all around her as Stacy and the pack left the tundra behind and immersed themselves into the new territory.

Do animals really live in this frozen biome? Stacy wondered. *And for that matter, has any human ever been here? Am I the first to explore this Arctic region?* The notion that Stacy could be the first human to step foot in the ice spikes made her lose her breath for a second. Stacy had never really given much thought to what she wanted to be when she grew up—her situation was unique since she lived with wolves in a forest instead of going to school like other kids her age. And she already had the job she always dreamed of, which was to be an animal rescuer. But if she had to choose another profession, explorer certainly seemed like a good option. She wondered how many places on the earth were still unexplored.

Everest and Addison led the group farther and farther into the ice spikes until they reached a clearing to rest for a while. Basil, Noah, and Wink were still full of energy, though. They began sprinting around the ice spikes, playing a fun game of tag. Everest and Addison seemed to be consulting each other on which direction they'd head next. Only Tucker seemed inclined to rest. He lay down on the ground and Stacy sat with her back leaning against his belly, watching as Basil, Noah, and Wink ran circles around them.

Suddenly, out of the corner of her eye, Stacy caught a glimpse of movement that was *not* one of her wolves. Peeking out from behind one of the ice spikes was something tiny and white . . . a wolf pup? *No! An Arctic fox!* Stacy didn't make any sound so she would not startle the small fox. She looked to Tucker, who had fallen asleep, and then to Addison and Everest, who were focused on a small map Addison had drawn in the ice. The others were still playing at the opposite end of the clearing, so Stacy got up and began slowly inching her way closer to the fox.

The fox was really small; it only came up to Stacy's shins. It was impossibly white and impossibly fluffy. It had deep black almond-shaped eyes and a black nose and whiskers that stood out in striking contrast against its white fur. Its tail was long and bushy with glimpses of a darker undercoat. *Of course,* Stacy thought. *You're exactly the type of animal who could live in this freezing biome.* The fox remained motionless as Stacy approached it. She crouched low to the ground so as not to appear threatening and avoided making eye contact with the small mammal.

Stacy couldn't help but be reminded of Page. She thought back to when she and her wolves had rescued Page and how Stacy initially thought Page was a fox based on her size, pointed ears, and her bushy tail. This fox looked just like Page, but white. Stacy reached her hand out and touched the top of the fox's head. Its fur was ten times softer than she imagined it would be.

"Hi, fella," Stacy cooed at the fox. The fox closed its eyes and leaned into Stacy's hand, savoring the affection.

All of a sudden, the fox had a burst of energy and began darting around Stacy playfully.

"Oh, you want to play, do you?" Stacy said with a smile. She stood up and began chasing the fox, who eagerly ran back and forth between Stacy's legs and looped around the ice spikes. Stacy turned in circles, trying to keep up with the fast fox. Minutes passed and Stacy, now winded, stopped spinning and looked around. All at once she was filled with dread because she realized she had no idea which direction she had come from when she followed the fox. All the ice spikes looked the same and the sky was an overcast gray—she couldn't use the sun to figure out which direction she was facing. The fox was ahead of her and seemed to be beckoning her to follow him. Stacy hoped he knew the direction back to her wolves.

Stacy had a hard time keeping up with the little fox, who seemed to know these ice spikes well. Stacy ran as fast as she could through the biome, squeezing through small holes in the ice that her wolves wouldn't be able to fit through. Stacy hoped they were shortcuts leading her back to her pack, but deep down she was growing more and more concerned that she might be lost. *And after I made that speech to Basil about not splitting up, I'm the one who goes off on her own and gets lost.*

Eventually, Stacy caught up to the fox, who had slowed down and was now sitting directly in the center of a ring of low ice spires. As she regained her breath, Stacy looked around and gasped—each one of the ice spires had a vertical row of symbols on it.

Did this fox lead me here? Can he read the runes too? Did he want me to see this? Stacy looked at the fox, who was now curled up asleep on the ice and snoring loudly, and then up at all the runes again.

"Addison!" Stacy called out into the cold air. "Come quick, I found something!"

THIRTEEN

NATURALLY, BASIL WAS the first wolf of Stacy's pack to answer her call. She came bounding into the clearing where Stacy and the fox were. Basil walked in a protective circle around Stacy, her head low, surveying for potential danger. She eased up once she realized Stacy was not in trouble.

Wink and Everest arrived next, followed seconds later by Addison, Noah, and Tucker. Addison noticed the runes instantly, without Stacy even needing to point them out to her. There were twelve of them spaced out in an almost perfect circle around the clearing. Addison spun around, looking at them several times each, as if she was searching for a beginning.

Wink and Tucker were standing over the Arctic fox now, who was still snoring loudly. The fox opened his eyes and looked up at the two curious wolves groggily. *Oh no,* Stacy thought. *The fox is going to be so scared the wolves might attack him that he'll run away for sure and I won't get to say good-bye.* Of course, Stacy wouldn't blame the fox for running away. To Stacy, Wink was a lovable goofball and Tucker was a giant, cuddly teddy bear. She easily forgot how formidable her wolves looked to other animals encountering them for the first time. To them, her wolves were apex predators to be feared. But the fox surprised Stacy. Instead of running away, he pressed his nose to Tucker's and then to Wink's to greet them and then (even more surprisingly) began playing with Wink.

Stacy turned her attention back to Addison and Everest, who were pacing around the clearing, taking in each rune before moving on to the next. *Is Addison teaching Everest to read them? Everest told me he couldn't read them. But maybe he can learn from Addison?*

Suddenly, the fox ran through Stacy's legs and around one of the ice spikes with a rune on it. Wink, who was chasing the fox, swerved to avoid crashing into Stacy, skidding past her on the ice and running headfirst into one of the spikes, causing a loud thud that echoed around the clearing.

"Wink, are you okay?" Stacy gasped, running over to a very dizzy Wink, who stood up and began stumbling around the clearing. Of course, Stacy knew he was all right—he was indestructible, after all. But he had hit his head pretty hard and it was Stacy's first instinct to be worried about him. "Wink, you need to be more carefu—"

C-C-C-R-R-R-A-A-A-C-C-C-K-K-K

Stacy glanced up at the spike Wink had crashed into and noticed a thin crack running up the spike and branching off in several directions. Fragments of ice began to rain down as the spike swayed back and forth as if it would crumble at any second. The other wolves and the fox instinctively took several steps back, their necks craned upward, looking at which direction the ice might fall, when the spike suddenly tipped forward, falling directly toward where Stacy was standing. Without hesitating, Wink charged Stacy, knocking her out of the way and taking the full impact of the huge ice shards as they crashed to the ground. He stood up and shook the ice rubble off him, as easily as if he was shaking off water droplets after a dip in the river back in the taiga.

"Wink!" Stacy shouted, jumping up and dusting herself off. "You saved me!" Tucker and Noah rubbed their heads against Wink, congratulating him. Everest had a disapproving expression, keenly aware that Wink had saved Stacy from a disaster of his own making.

Addison, however, seemed distraught, and Stacy quickly realized why. The rune that was on the ice spike was now in pieces all around them. *Oh no. She might not be able to make sense of all of the symbols with one of them missing. If only I had sketched the runes before Wink broke one of them.* Stacy sketched all of them quickly, except for the missing spike.

Addison began frantically sifting through the ice pile, looking for pieces of the runes. Stacy and the others helped her, and they were able to pull out two symbols, although Stacy could not remember which order they had been in on the ice spike.

"Addison, I found another!" Stacy shouted as Addison and Everest were positioning the other two in the center of the clearing. Basil helped Stacy pull it over to where the others were. Stacy stepped back and looked at the three symbols.

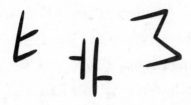

Addison studied them briefly and then began searching again. Stacy surmised that there must be another rune missing and resumed her search, turning over every piece of loose ice till her fingers were frozen and needed to be warmed by Tucker. It was Noah who finally found the missing piece and pulled it out. Stacy, the other wolves, and the fox walked over and looked at the symbol. Stacy had seen this one before, but still had no idea what it meant.

Addison, however, did. She barked and the little fox ran over to her. It seemed to Stacy that Addison was asking the fox a question—the way they kept pointing their noses in different directions and nodding. Eventually, their snouts were both pointed in the same direction, sniffing the cold wind, and the other wolves gathered around. The little fox ran over to Stacy and brushed up against her leg. As much as Stacy didn't want to accept it, she knew this was good-bye. She knelt down and put her arms around the fox. *I'll miss you. Stay safe.*

"We're not like normal humans and wolves," she whispered to the fox. "You would do well to avoid anyone else who comes into your home. But thank you for befriending us."

The fox gave Stacy one last nuzzle and then scampered off. Basil came up behind Stacy and motioned for her to climb on her back. Before Stacy knew what was happening, the pack left the circle of runes and were running quickly until suddenly they reached the end of the ice-spike forest. Stacy saw what was now in front of them—a giant glacier.

The glacier was like a mountain, with a cliffside that was sixty feet tall and jagged peaks near the top. From what Stacy could see, it stretched for at least a mile to the southwest along the tundra. To the northeast, it gave way to arctic ocean waters. And at the bottom of the giant glacier was a small, singular cave opening. Addison strode confidently toward it. Stacy exchanged a nervous glance with Everest. *Did Addi know about this cave? Did the rune tell her to come this way? Is this where all our travels across the tundra have been leading us?*

"Um, Addi," Stacy said nervously. "You don't actually want to . . ." Stacy's voice trailed off. She was going to ask Addison if she wanted to go in the glacier cave, but Addison had already disappeared inside it.

Yes, of course that's what you want to do, Stacy thought as she hopped off Basil's back and raced after Addison into the darkness.

FOURTEEN

STACY RAN AFTER Addison into the cave. Even when the light began to disappear behind her, she kept going—finding her footing in the dark. It was only when it became pitch black that she stopped running, reached into her bag for her flint and steel, and lit a torch. Stacy gasped. The glacier cave was no ordinary cave. From the outside, it may have looked unassuming, but inside it was . . . a cavern. A gargantuan ice cavern—with tunnels branching off in different directions and, in the center, an intricate life-size ice carving of a wolf. Stacy walked up to the ice statue and ran her fingers along its cold, smooth back. It was spooky how much the statue resembled Everest—large, strong . . . alpha. Toward the back of the palatial room, there was a table carved into the ice. Upon it were several ice-carving tools, including a shiny pickaxe, and a leather-bound journal. Stacy opened the journal. The leather cover was stiff and frozen. Inside were pages and pages of the symbols she'd seen in the snow and on the ice spikes. Stacy looked up around at the walls and let out a tiny gasp; they too were completely covered with runes.

"Addison?" she whispered. "Addi, where are you?"

Stacy looked behind her to see if any of her other wolves had followed her, but it seemed she was alone. They were probably waiting for her to call out that it was safe. Stacy imagined Noah and Wink holding Everest back to keep him from charging in to protect her. Everest was so strong that Basil and Tucker would probably need to help restrain him too. Stacy was nervous, but she smiled at the thought as she walked deeper into the rows of ice wolves, eventually turning a corner to another room.

"Oh, Addison." Stacy breathed heavily. "I found you."

Addison was standing in front of a large wall that was covered in runes. Stacy held her torch up to them.

There were four rows, each containing seven symbols, except for the bottom row, which had only five. Stacy thought back to the one encyclopedia book she had in the cave . . . the letter H, and about how she had pored over the entry for "Hieroglyphics." She was fascinated by the civilizations of the Egyptians, but these markings did not look like any of the hieroglyphics she saw pictured in her book. Still, there was something about the runes that reminded Stacy of them. *It must be some type of ancient language. When we get back to the taiga, I should go to the village library and figure out what culture used this language.*

Stacy looked up at the giant wall of runes. This was definitely the largest amount of them she'd seen together so far. Addison gave her a look that seemed to say, *These ones are important.* Not wanting to forget them, Stacy gave Addison the torch to hold in her mouth and pulled her notebook and pen from her satchel and sketched the wall of runes. When she was done, she took the torch back from Addison.

"I'm going to go get the others," Stacy said. "They need to see this."

Addison gave her a nod and then moved to the next chamber, which contained even more rune murals. Stacy made her way back through the room with the wolf statue and back up the sloping entrance to the front of the glacier where the other wolves in her pack were waiting. Everest was pacing back and forth right at the entrance to the ice cave while Noah and Basil were lapping up water from a puddle Tucker must have melted for them. Tucker was curled up resting and Wink was lying on his side, completely asleep with his tongue hanging out.

"Addison's fine," Stacy said, while catching her breath. Wink woke up and he and the other wolves gathered around Stacy. "This is it. This is where she's been leading us. I'm not sure what it is really, but you should all come with me and see it for yourselves."

Everest, Tucker, Noah, Basil, and Wink followed Stacy down to where Addison was, their eyes widening more and more with every new sight in the cavern. Seeing Everest side by side with the ice wolf was an eerie sight. The group pressed on, deeper into the cavern, until they caught up with Addison, who they took turns greeting. *Aww, they must have been worried about her,* Stacy thought. Now that they were all reunited as a pack, the wolves turned to face Stacy, awaiting her instructions.

"We keep going," Stacy said in a firm tone. "Let's explore the rest of this place. We've come this far, after all. Addison, that's what you want, isn't it?"

Addison nodded and Stacy felt safe knowing that Addison didn't think they were in danger. If anything, there was something familiar about this place. Not that Stacy had ever been here before—she was sure she hadn't. But the energy of the place, the wolf ice statue that looked like Everest, the symbols that Addison magically knew how to read, the Arctic fox that looked like Page who led Stacy to the runes in the ice spikes—it was as if they were meant to come here. *How crazy is that? A couple of weeks ago, the idea of mounting an expedition to the tundra would have seemed preposterous. And now we're here and it feels like we were supposed to come here all along. . . .*

"This place . . ." Stacy said to the wolves in a hushed voice. "Have you been here before?"

She looked around at her wolves. Wink was shaking his head no. But Addison, Tucker, Basil, and Noah were looking at Everest, whose face bore a wistful expression Stacy had never seen before. He made no gesture of a yes or a no, but rather looked around the room, as if he was trying to remember.

"It's familiar to you, isn't it?" Stacy said. Everest nodded slowly. Stacy and the others sat for a few seconds in silence.

"I think this could be where you're from," Stacy said finally. The wolves all exchanged nervous looks with one another. "Let's keep going then. I want to find some answers."

Stacy led the wolves to the next room, a smaller chamber with a spiral staircase carved into the ice that seemed to lead down to a lower level. Holding the torch in front of her, they began to descend. The staircase was long—longer than Stacy thought possible. They reached the bottom and saw that they were now at the end of a narrow corridor. And at the very end of the corridor, a dim light flickered in a small room. *Is there someone there?*

Basil leaned over Stacy's shoulder and blew out the torch. Everest positioned himself at the front of the pack, with Addison behind him. Tucker, Basil, Noah, and Wink formed a protective barrier around Stacy and, together, they began to make their way down the hall. They walked slowly, trying to make as little noise as possible. *There's something at the end of this hallway,* Stacy thought as they crept in silence. *It might be dangerous, but if it is, I know my wolves will protect me.*

In the darkness, Stacy trained her eyes on Everest, straining to see the wolf's face as he was the first to enter the dimly lit room. His expression was fierce and defensive, but softened as the amber light washed across his face and he took in their surroundings. The only way Stacy could think to describe the room was "magical." The ceiling was comprised of crystal stalactites that hung down to just above Stacy's head. They were a translucent, milky white with flecks of sparkly blue and amethyst. There was a small fire in the center of the room that had burned down to cinders. But as soon as Stacy and the wolves drew near, it roared back to life.

Stacy looked over at Everest and saw his expression

had turned to one of pity. A second later, Stacy understood why. As she entered deeper into the room behind
Addison, she saw him. A lone and feeble wolf, lying on
the floor in the corner.

The first thing Stacy noticed about the old wolf was
his eyes. They were glassy and gray, with a hint of dull
purple to them. His fur was scraggly and coarse, and
he had long wiry whiskers that protruded from either
side of his lean snout. But his eyes—his eyes looked like
they'd seen a hundred years go by and could tell a thou-
sand stories. He blinked slowly, and every time he did
Stacy wondered if he was closing his eyes for a nap. But
then they'd snap back open, and she was mesmerized by
his gaze once more.

Everest was the first to approach him. He walked over
to where the wolf was lying, gave him a slight bow, and
then lay down in front of him so that they were nose-
to-nose. The elder wolf stared into Everest's silver eyes.
Everest's eyes flickered and moved around, as if he was
watching something. Occasionally Everest would nod
and sometimes his expression would change from sad
to understanding. When he was finished, the elder wolf
laid his head down on the ground and closed his eyes to
rest. *Was the elder wolf communicating with Everest just*

then? Can he talk to Everest the same way I can talk to him with my thoughts?

Stacy wasn't sure, but one thing was clear to her. She felt it as soon as she entered the room, deep in her soul, and she wished more than anything that it wasn't true.

The elder wolf was dying.

FIFTEEN

STACY HAD A theory. It had entered her mind as soon as she saw the elder wolf conversing with Everest using telepathy. She gathered her pack outside of the wolf's chambers so she could share her theory with them.

"He has all of your powers," Stacy told the pack. "He knows how to read and write in symbols, since the cavern is full of them. He can also communicate with his mind like Everest. And I'm pretty sure he started a fire when we first entered the room, just like Basil can."

The wolves all looked around to each other, considering Stacy's theory.

"I suspect he's indestructible like Wink, which is how

he's managed to live to such an old age," Stacy continued. "And he can probably breathe underwater like Noah . . . but of course, there's no way to test that."

Tucker took a step toward Stacy as if to say, *What about me?*

"Tucker, you have the ability to heal others . . . ," Stacy said. "But have you ever actually healed *yourself*?" Tucker looked flummoxed. "The elder wolf can likely heal others too, like you. But I wonder if maybe he can't heal himself. Which is why I fear that he's . . . going to die soon."

The wolves hung their heads in sadness. It was clear that not only did they believe Stacy's theory, but they also agreed with her that the elder wolf's time was short. Tears rolled down Stacy's cheeks and fell onto the floor of the icy corridor. Something else was troubling Stacy though. *Why is this wolf here all alone? Where are the other members of his pack? Surely he had a pack, right? Could it be that he is the last of his generation? Have the other members of his pack all died?*

Stacy suspected Everest knew the answers to these questions from when the elder wolf had relayed his story to him, but there was no way for Everest to tell Stacy. Suddenly, Tucker broke away from where the pack was standing and walked back into the elder wolf's chambers. He lay down near the wolf, who was still resting from expending energy communicating with Everest. Stacy suspected Tucker was going to try to heal him. Noah brought some water in a small bowl and set it near the elder wolf's mouth. Everest and Addison positioned themselves in front of the elder wolf, seemingly determined to glean as much information from him as they could.

This left Stacy, Wink, and Basil without tasks. The room was crowded, though, so Stacy suggested they wander around the cavern some more and clear out of the other wolves' way for a bit while they tended to the elder wolf. Basil pressed her nose to Stacy's torch, reigniting its flame, and the three of them set off deeper into the ice cavern. Stacy wasn't sure what they would find wandering around, but she knew they'd only be getting in the way if they stayed back with the elder wolf.

The three of them walked back down the long corridor to the spiral staircase. They headed upstairs and into the large rooms with murals on the walls. Stacy wanted to copy as many of the rune passages into her notebook as she could. She was determined to eventually find some way of reading them. But if for some reason that wasn't possible, she at least wanted Addison to have the option to read them again when they were back home at the cave.

Basil headed outside to go for a run. Practically speaking, Stacy knew that Basil would scout the area and determine which routes were safe to take when the time came to head back home, but Stacy also knew that Basil liked to run to clear her mind when something was bothering her. Stacy sensed Basil's desire to run right now had more to do with taking her mind off the dying elder wolf than scouting.

Stacy spent several hours sketching the runes with Wink at her side. Her hand grew cold and cramped from drawing so many of the runes in her notebook. She flipped through the rune-filled pages. The language looked beautiful, but she longed to know what it meant. Basil returned from her run and Stacy decided enough time had passed that they should go back downstairs to check on how everyone was doing.

Stacy, Basil, and Wink tiptoed (or in Basil and Wink's case, tip-pawed) through the archway of the elder wolf's chambers so as not to disturb him in case he was sleeping. As they approached the others, Stacy saw that the old wolf was, in fact, asleep. Everest and Addison looked weary, fatigued from keeping vigil at the wolf's bedside for several hours. Noah was curled up near the fire and Tucker, *poor Tucker*, was still at the wolf's side, trying in vain to heal him. Stacy suspected Tucker's healing abilities would not be able to help the old wolf—that he was too far gone and that it was his time to die. She also suspected that deep down, Tucker knew this too. But Stacy also understood Tucker needed to try everything he could.

"Why don't you all go up for some fresh air," Stacy said, breaking the silence in the room. "Wink and I can keep watch for a bit. We can send Basil up to get you quickly if anything happens."

One by one, the wolves got up and filed out of the room past Stacy. Everest was the first, and Stacy gave him a kiss on the cheek as he passed by her. He was followed by Addison and Noah and, lastly, a dejected-looking Tucker.

"You're doing everything you can for him," Stacy said to the wolves as they started down the corridor. "I'm sure he knows that and is appreciative."

Stacy turned back to the elder wolf. She wanted so badly to approach him, but she had kept her distance thus far. *Who knows if he's ever seen a human before in his entire life? He might not want me here.* Stacy decided she would put her doubts aside, and knelt down near the elder wolf, cupping his muzzle in her hands.

The elder wolf stirred, lifting his head and pressing his nose to Stacy's. What happened next, Stacy could only describe as having some type of dream . . . or vision. Purple light flashed before her eyes and suddenly she was upstairs in the room with the wolf ice sculpture. A man sat on a stool, working on the ice carving while a tiny wolf pup poked his head out from behind the statue. He stood below it, looking up at the statue in progress, and puffed his chest out to mimic its fierce stance. The man paused his work to look down at the pup adoringly. Something about the small wolf was familiar to Stacy. *Everest?* The purple light flashed again, and Stacy was transported this time to the tundra just outside of the ice cave. A beautiful wolf was standing alongside a woman. The wolf's coat was white and gray like Everest's, with patches of rust-colored fur along her back like Addison's. Her fur was thick like Tucker's, fluffy like Noah's, and shiny like Basil's. Her eyes were prismatic. Suddenly, a male wolf with vibrant purple eyes emerged from the cave with five small wolf puppies following him. The purple light flashed again. Stacy was back in one of the cave's chambers where the woman sat at a desk, writing in symbols. A tiny wolf slept in her lap with one eye closed particularly tightly. *Wink?* Purple light enveloped Stacy again and the vision dissipated.

Stacy opened her eyes and looked around her. Everest, Tucker, and Addison had returned, and all of her wolves were looking at Stacy with concerned expressions.

"Everest was here as a wolf pup," Stacy blurted out. "Wink too. You all were. You're all the descendants of the wolves who lived here. They're your ancestors."

Stacy looked at the dying wolf. He was exhausted from showing Stacy the past. Everest and Tucker were beside him and, looking at them and then back to the old wolf, Stacy could only imagine how hardy and full of life the elder wolf must have been in his youth.

Tucker began to glow, channeling all his energy into

one final attempt to heal the dying wolf. But it was no use. The elder wolf drew his final breath. Tucker let out a sorrowful howl that reverberated through the glacier walls. Stacy cried on Wink's shoulder and Addison comforted Everest while Noah and Basil looked on in horror. Tucker's howl was still echoing throughout the chamber. But then came a different sound. Stacy heard what sounded like glass shattering all around her. She looked for the source of the noise, but she saw nothing. The stalactites on the ceiling, however, began to quiver and tiny cracks began to form on the walls around them. All at once, Stacy and the others realized what was happening.

"RUN!" Stacy shouted over the growing rumble above them. "The glacier is collapsing!"

SIXTEEN

NOAH AND ADDISON were the first to race out of the room and down the crumbling corridor. Everest stood in the doorway of the elder wolf's chambers, ready to protect Stacy should the roof cave in.

"Go with the others!" Stacy shouted to Everest. His silver eyes were wide with panic. "Make sure the way out is clear, I'll be right behind!"

Everest motioned to Basil and Wink to stay with Stacy and then ran off after the others to clear the way. Stacy looked at Tucker, who was shielding the elder wolf's body from the small, but sharp, ice daggers that were breaking off the stalactites and raining down on them.

"Tucker doesn't want to leave him down here!" Stacy shouted to Basil over the noise of the shifting ice above them. Wink ran over to Tucker and tried to pull him away from the elder wolf.

"Tuck!" Stacy shouted. "This is where he wanted to die. He would want his body to stay here. You have to come with us now . . . PLEASE!"

Tucker nodded slowly and started to stand, but his legs buckled under him and he collapsed onto the floor. Stacy ran over to him.

"He's depleted from trying to heal the elder wolf!" Stacy shouted to Wink, who raced to Tucker's side. Basil and Stacy lifted Tucker onto Wink's back and then Wink set off into the corridor while Stacy climbed on Basil. She wrapped both of her arms around the wolf's neck for what she assumed was going to be a very fast, very bumpy sprint to the surface. Stacy gave the elder wolf one last look before Basil took off like a bolt of lightning, passing Wink and Tucker in the corridor, Everest on the staircase (which was swaying back and forth as the glacier moved), and then finally overtaking Addison and Noah in the hall with the ice statue, which was now in shattered pieces on the ground.

"Basil, stop!" Stacy shouted, jumping off the wolf

and grabbing the pickaxe and diary from the crumbling ice desk. They raced out of the entrance and onto the tundra just in time to turn around and see the giant glacier shift and slide into a new position, demolishing everything in its path and creating a giant wave of water beneath it that spilled out over the tundra.

Stacy and the wolves stood a safe distance away watching, and grieved in silence over the elder wolf's death. Stacy knew they all wished they could have spent more time with him, but she was grateful for everything they'd experienced in the precious hours they had together. Stacy thought about how lucky they were to have arrived when they did. But no sooner had she had the thought than Everest nudged her shoulder with his nose. Stacy turned to him and the alpha wolf shook his head no. *What do you mean, Everest? If we had arrived a day later than we did, the elder wolf would have already passed away, and we wouldn't have learned what we did from him. Unless . . . did he wait for us to get here before he died?* Stacy hadn't considered the fact that the elder wolf might have been using his powers to delay his death until they reached him. He must have journeyed out on the tundra to leave the runes in the ice that Addison found. He was hoping someone would make it to the cavern before he passed away.

Stacy turned her attention to Tucker, who was standing next to her but looked like he'd tip over if Stacy so much as tapped him.

"Sit down, boy," Stacy said worriedly.

Tucker obeyed and sat down. The other wolves huddled around him, instantly concerned about their pack member. It was clear that Tucker had overexerted himself trying to heal the elder wolf. He needed to rest.

Daylight was dwindling and Basil lit a fire in remembrance of the elder wolf. Stacy and the wolves sat in a circle around it, reflecting on the experience they'd all shared. Even though they'd only known him for a very short time, watching the elder wolf die and the collapse of his ice home felt like a tremendous loss to Stacy and the others. It reminded Stacy of when she'd seen Dusky perish in the forest fire at the taiga. Seeing a wolf die was something Stacy would not wish on anyone. She'd seen it twice now and she never wanted to witness something like that again in her life. The elder wolf's passing was even more upsetting though, because now Stacy knew the elder wolf was a direct relative of her pack—possibly even their father! If only her wolves had been able to have more time with him. Stacy was thankful, though, for the visions that both she and Everest had experienced and for all the murals on the wall that Addison had been able to take in and that Stacy had sketched in her notebook.

Stars filled the night sky as Basil's fire for the elder wolf continued to burn. Stacy looked up and noticed the sky was green and purple. It looked so magical. *The aurora borealis! I've read about this phenomenon in the sky before, but I never thought I'd actually get to see it with my own eyes! It's beautiful. I bet that's the spirit of the elder wolf up there in the sky now watching over us.*

Stacy wiped a tear from her face and looked around at the others. Basil, Everest, and Noah were looking up at the sky in wonder. Wink was sneaking some fish out of the pack Everest was wearing. Tucker was resting peacefully. Stacy noticed that Addison was looking behind them above the glacier with a concerned look on her face. Stacy spun around and gasped. A huge storm was forming over the glacier and moving toward them.

"We need to find shelter," Stacy said. But with the ice cavern no longer there, the pack had limited options. Stacy looked around the tundra, but she knew they wouldn't be able to find anything before the storm reached them.

"What if we . . . *built* something?" Stacy asked. Addison spun around in circles and barked excitedly. "We could build an igloo!"

Stacy had seen pictures of an igloo before and knew they would need some snow bricks in order to build one. The snow on the ground of the tundra was pretty compacted and Stacy thought it should work well for building an igloo. She picked up the pickaxe from the cave and held it to the ground.

"Here goes nothing," she said, holding onto the heavy tool with both hands. Stacy clumsily sliced through the tundra, creating a large rectangular brick of icy snow that Noah and Everest helped her lift out and place down on a flat patch of ground nearby. They repeated this process close to fifty times, with Addison guiding them to where they should place each new brick Stacy cut from the snow, until they had built a crude igloo. It was nothing Stacy could have ever managed on her own. She knew that igloo-building skills were passed down generation to generation among cultures such as the Inuit. But for it being her first time using this pickaxe and building it with a bunch of wolves . . . she had to admit she was rather impressed with herself.

The snow had started to fall halfway through building the igloo. At first it was pretty and it helped Stacy and the wolves to fill and smooth over the cracks in the igloo. But as they were finishing their build, the wind picked up and blew the snow in all directions around them. Stacy's face stung from the hard wind and her fingers were numb.

"Quick!" Stacy shouted. "Everyone inside!"

Stacy and the wolves entered through the small tunnel-like opening in the front. That was Addison's idea. It was a feature in traditional igloos meant to stop the wind from blowing in and to help trap some of the heat.

Inside the igloo, Stacy and the other wolves were cozy. *Very* cozy. They hadn't had time to build an igloo large enough to fit all six wolves comfortably for very long. With Stacy inside, everyone was touching each other. The wind howled loudly and Stacy suspected the center of the snowstorm was upon them now. She glanced at the igloo walls nervously.

"Hopefully this holds through the night. . . ."

SEVENTEEN

STACY WOKE TO a gentle nuzzling from Tucker. She was relieved to see Tucker was feeling better and to discover that their igloo had stood up to the snowstorm and that they'd all survived the night. Stacy crawled out of the igloo. The cloudless sky was bright blue. The storm had passed. Stacy stretched her arms up to the sky and took some deep breaths. She smelled . . . fish. Addison and Noah were cooking up some salmon while Wink looked on hungrily. Everest and Basil were a few hundred yards away from the igloo, likely charting the direction the pack would head next.

The pack was quiet during breakfast. Everyone was

still heavy-hearted from the events of the day before. They packed up camp, and Everest motioned for them all to head west. Stacy climbed on Wink's back and the group set off. *Where are we going now that Addison is no longer leading us to the elder wolf's ice home? Does Everest have a plan for where we should go now?*

Suddenly, and without warning, Everest camouflaged with the tundra. All the other wolves' fur bristled and changed appearance as well, leaving Stacy riding a nearly invisible wolf. Wink ran to a boulder and crouched behind it, lowering Stacy to the ground.

Stacy peered around the boulder and saw what the problem was. A giant helicopter was on the tundra about two hundred yards away from them, its blades still in rotation, but its rails on the ground. There were already people outside of the helicopter, walking around on the snow.

"Dr. Berg!" A female voice echoed across the tundra. "Over here, I've already found some wolf tracks."

"Very good," Dr. Berg replied, stepping out of the helicopter. "Your semester in the field is off to a good start already." Dr. Berg was tall and lanky and had a thin nose and wore spectacles. His long red hair was tied in a low ponytail.

Dr. Berg walked over to the female researcher, who

Stacy noticed was carrying a tranquilizer gun, and inspected the tracks. Stacy wondered if they were actually her wolves' tracks from a few days ago. One of Stacy's wolves, she wasn't sure which, came up to her and nudged her to climb on their back. Stacy typically only rode on Wink or Basil, and this wolf's movements were graceful and steady, not at all gangly. *This must be Basil.* Stacy climbed on and held tight. Basil waited until the researcher and Dr. Berg had their backs turned to them and then she shot off in the opposite direction like a bolt of lightning, putting as much distance between Stacy and the other humans as she could in just a few seconds.

When she could no longer see the humans or the helicopter, Basil slowed to let Stacy down. Her camouflage was wearing off. *Hmm,* Stacy thought. *Everest must only be able to extend his powers to the other wolves within a certain radius.* What that radius was, Stacy had no idea. But now the other wolves had caught up to her and Basil and everyone was visible again. They kept walking and Stacy thought about what a close call that had been.

They were in a helicopter flying over the tundra. They could have easily spotted our igloo or one of our fires. They could have tranquilized one of my wolves from the sky and then what would we have done? But now the pack was safe.

"Wait!" Stacy said, stopping in her tracks. "Don't you all know what this means?"

Addison obviously was thinking exactly what Stacy was thinking. Her tail was wagging and she was nodding at Stacy. The other wolves looked befuddled.

"If Dr. Berg and his team are here . . . ," Stacy started, "then that means they aren't back in the taiga. We can go home!"

All of the wolves' tails began wagging and Wink spun around in celebratory circles. Stacy danced around with him until he stopped long enough for her to hop on his back.

"Mush!" Stacy yelled. The wolves looked at her with blank expressions. "I read that was some type of dogsled command. Never mind. Not a moment to lose. Let's go home! To the taiga!"

The pack changed directions and started running south toward the mountain range they'd first summited that led them to the tundra at the beginning of the expedition.

Stacy pulled out her binoculars from her satchel and scanned the mountain range, looking for either a pass or the least daunting peak for them to summit. As the wolves began climbing up the mountain in front of them, Stacy's eyes caught a glimpse of movement high up on one of the craggy overhangs. *Is it a snowshoe hare?* *No! A lynx cub! Is it alone?*

Everest, hearing Stacy's thoughts, also looked up to where the cub was precariously crouched. He let out a stern bark. *Everest, no! We have to rescue it if it's all alone. I know it's dangerous, but that's what we do! Besides, you all have so many more new powers than you did before. We can handle it.*

The group made their way up toward the small lynx until the mountain was too steep to continue. Stacy hopped off Wink's back and pulled her pickaxe out from where it was tucked on her satchel strap. Everest took a step forward.

"Okay," Stacy said. "Everest will come with me up the mountain to rescue the lynx cub. Basil and Wink should come too. Addison and Noah can stay behind with Tucker so he can get some rest."

Stacy, Everest, Basil, and Wink began their ascent up the overhang. Stacy used her pickaxe to dig into the ice above her and then pull herself up and find stable footing so she could pull her pickaxe out of the ice and repeat the process again. It was hard work, but after about twenty minutes or so, she looked up and saw that they weren't too far from the cub. Everest was in front of Stacy. She grabbed onto him to pull herself up the steepest part of the overhang. Now, standing on top of it, they looked back to where Basil and Wink were a few yards below them.

"Wait there," Stacy called back to them. "We'll grab the cub and come back!"

Stacy and Everest inched their way closer to where the cub was cowering, but the snow was loose and they had a hard time wading through it. The cub weighed so little it sat on top of the snow, shivering. Stacy looked at the cub now that they were closer to it. Its fur was sticking out every which way and it had giant ears and whiskers that it would likely need to grow into. There were little black tufts of hair that stood up above its ears, forming tiny triangles. Its nose was pastel pink and its fur was mostly white with hints of gray and taupe stripes.

All of a sudden, the snow began to shift underneath Stacy's feet. She looked up to Everest, who was also moving back and forth with the snow. There was no time to lose. Stacy grabbed the cub and tucked it into her satchel as the snow continued to move all around her feet. *Oh no*, Stacy thought. *I know what's happening. This could be deadly.*

"Avalanche!!!!"

EIGHTEEN

"HHHEELLLPPPP!" STACY SHOUTED at the top of her lungs as she slid down the mountainside. She was helpless against the power of the avalanche. Everest had also been swept up in it and together they careened away from the wolf pack and down the mountain.

Stacy, Everest, and the cub fell for several hundred feet before hitting bottom. Stacy was sucked under the snow as if she was caught in the current of a fast-moving river. She felt herself drifting apart from Everest and sliding deeper and deeper under the cascading snow. Suddenly, everything around her stopped moving. Stacy had stopped moving. She was trapped in the

stillness—suspended in the snow, unable to tell which way was up or down. An eerie calm rushed over her . . . and then fear. The avalanche was over, and she hadn't been hurt or broken any bones. But her current situation was worse—she was buried under at least thirty feet of snow and would run out of oxygen in minutes. . . .

I'm going to die, Stacy thought to herself. *We're going to die.* Her arms were pinned to her sides, but she was able to reach down into her satchel and stroke the warm cub's tiny head. It stirred, too weak to do much else, and Stacy could feel the vibrations of its purrs against her fingertips. A tear crept out of the corner of one of Stacy's eyes and instantly froze on her cheek. *Where's Everest? Is this really the end for me?* She closed her eyes and thought of the happiest memory she could. She thought about her life in the taiga with the wolves and how good it had been. She thought about Page and Molly and how much she loved them and would miss taking them for outings in the taiga and playing hide-and-seek. . . .

I'm sorry, Everest. We always knew one of our animal rescues might end up this way. Remember the time I rescued a rabbit at the top of a waterfall? You thought I took too big a risk then. But I did it anyway. Just like I took too big a risk rescuing Page near the lava. Just like the risk I took saving Molly in the slot canyon in the mesa. And just like this rescue. Please don't blame yourself. It's not your fault. Tell all the other wolves I love them. Tell Tucker there was no way for him to save me from this. And tell Basil it wasn't her fault either. Please look after Page, Molly, and Milquetoast. Keep them safe. And keep rescuing animals. And have a great life in the taiga. Don't forget about me. I'll never forget you. You changed my life, Everest.

The tiny cub squirmed inside Stacy's bag, breaking her train of thought. Stacy couldn't bear the thought of it suffocating. She reached inside her bag to comfort it and felt it give a small kick at the bottom of her satchel. Stacy reached down and felt something cold. *What is it? Did some snow get in?* Stacy had snow in her boots, her eyes, her ears . . . it was everywhere. She felt around and her fingers brushed up against something cold and hard. *A rock?* No—it was her whistle!

Stacy couldn't believe it. She almost hadn't packed it. Everest had found the whistle in the woods one day when Stacy had first come to live with them; he'd given it to her in case they were ever separated.

Stacy knew Everest was racing against time to find her at this very moment. He knew she was lost, trapped, but Stacy had no way of describing where she was. Everything was just . . . white. But with a whistle— with a whistle she might just have a chance. Wolves have excellent hearing and Everest should be able to pinpoint her location with her blowing it. Stacy clasped her fingers around the whistle, the cub still squirming a bit in her bag. She went to bring the whistle to her lips to blow, but quickly realized she couldn't lift her arms. The snow had her trapped. Stacy began digging with her fingers, trying to loosen the packed snow around her wrists (and eventually her elbow), until she was holding the whistle to her chest. She bent her head down—her lips pursed. She wiggled around until, at last, she had her mouth around the flat part of the whistle.

Stacy took a deep breath in, not knowing how many more full breaths she'd be able to take. She blew but no sound came out. There was snow in the whistle! Thinking fast, Stacy took the whole whistle in her mouth, sucking out the snow. She then pushed it out of her mouth and blew three short blasts. The sound was weak at first and Stacy knew it was now or never. She had to blow the whistle as hard as she could to try to save her and the cub. *One . . . two . . . three . . . four . . . five . . . six . . . seven.* She got seven more blows of the whistle, each slightly louder than the last, until she ran out of breath. The whistle dropped into her hand and Stacy started panting, her breathing very shallow. That was her last hope.

And then, she heard a faint scratching noise coming from above her. . . .

Suddenly, bright light flooded in all around her, causing Stacy to blink rapidly. A hole above her opened up and she saw Noah, furiously digging down to where Stacy was trapped. *Of course! Noah's the perfect wolf to search through the avalanche because he never needs to come up for air!*

"Noah!" Stacy called out to him. "Boy, am I glad to see you!"

Noah continued to dig furiously around Stacy, loosening the snow so she could stand and had room to move her arms around. She gave Noah a big hug and then looked up at least a hundred feet to the tiny hole of bright blue sky above them. *How are we ever going to get up there?* Just then, Everest popped his head into the hole, covering up the sky.

"Everest!" Stacy shouted up. "I'm so happy you're okay!"

Everest tossed down the pack's climbing rope, which Noah used to tie a triple fisherman's knot around Stacy's waist. He gave a tug on the rope, indicating to Everest that he could begin to pull.

Everest, who was without question the strongest wolf in Stacy's pack, pulled her, the cub, and Noah all the way to the surface. Stacy rolled over on her back, panting heavily and relieved to finally be above the snow. As soon as Stacy regained her breath, she checked on the cub, fearing the worst. *It's alive!* They'd made it out and survived an avalanche, one of nature's most powerful displays of force.

Stacy got to her feet and wobbled a bit to one side, her muscles weak from being trapped under heavy snow for so long. Everest and Noah walked on either side of her so she could hang her arms over both of their backs for support. Together, they carefully made their way through the newly deposited snowbanks to the cliff where Stacy could see some of the other wolves waiting.

"Wink, Addi, Tucker, Basil . . . good, you're all okay," Stacy said wearily. Wink nodded enthusiastically, while Addison and Basil nodded more slowly. *Of course Wink is all right*, Stacy thought to herself. *Nothing can kill him— he probably thought the avalanche was great fun! Basil and Addison must have had a pretty hard time getting Tucker out of there in his weakened condition. I'm so happy we're all okay—that could have ended really, really badly.*

Stacy reached into her pack and pulled out the cub. Addison, Basil, and Wink huddled around it, taking turns to get a close look at the tiny fuzzball. When they were done, Stacy brought the cub over to where Tucker was lying. She knelt down and placed the lynx cub down between his paws and he immediately began to nuzzle and groom it. The cub closed its eyes in delight and began purring loudly.

"Aww, fast friends," Stacy said to Tucker and the cub. "You guys are good for each other." Tucker had such wonderful motherly instincts and Stacy could tell the cub was already beginning to perk up.

Stacy stood up and surveyed the pack's surroundings. The avalanche had caused her to lose all sense of direction and it took her a minute to get her bearings. The avalanche had pushed them pretty far down the mountain away from the tundra. Stacy looked to the south and saw that there were patches of ground without snow. They were on the complete other side of the mountain range now, which meant . . . *Could it be that we're already almost* . . . Stacy looked into the distance where there was no snow, but rather towering spruce trees with dark brown trunks and dark green leafy tops way up in the sky.

The taiga!

NINETEEN

THE PACK RACED toward the familiar skyline of the taiga. Some of the wolves let out celebratory barks as they ran. Basil zoomed between spruce trees, running excited circles around her other pack members. Stacy held the cub close and breathed in the fresh forest fragrances. Spring was in full swing—orange tulips and white daisies were blooming, birds were chirping, and the air smelled sweet.

"This is where we're from," she whispered to the cub. "This is home."

I wonder if Milquetoast will like that I'm bringing home

a lynx? Hopefully he'll enjoy having another member of the feline family in the cave so it's not just him and the dogs. This lynx cub is weak though—I should go to the village veterinarian and get some formula for it to eat for a few days to regain its strength. Then I'm going to weave it and Milquetoast some baskets to sleep in. . . .

Stacy's thoughts were interrupted by the sound of wings fluttering by her ear. She looked up to see Milo the bat zooming alongside her and Wink.

"It's good to see you, Milo," Stacy said. "Let all the bats know we're back and available for animal rescues, will ya?"

Milo flew off in the direction of the cave, leaving Stacy to wonder what animal would need rescuing the next time she saw the tiny brown bat. She hoped there had been no animals that needed their help while they were away.

The wolves slowed from a run to a walk. Stacy hopped off Wink and set the cub down on the ground while she took off her jacket and tied it around her waist. The cub was just a little taller than the red-and-white-spotted toadstool it was standing next to. Stacy smiled and scooped it back up and tucked it into her satchel where the cub happily sat, its head poking out of the top flap, looking up with wide eyes at the giant trees in the taiga.

Page and Molly were waiting in the clearing outside the cave as the wolves approached. Stacy guessed that Milo must have alerted Page to their homecoming. Molly ran around in frantic circles and barked, while Page ran to Stacy as soon as she saw her. Stacy knelt down and happily accepted Page's sloppy kisses until Molly ran over, and then Stacy used both her hands to scratch behind Molly's and Page's ears.

"I missed you both so much!" Stacy exclaimed.

Suddenly, Page jerked her head up and cocked it to one side, her nose twitching. Stacy was expecting this. Nervously, Stacy reached into her bag and pulled out the fluffy cub, bracing herself for a bad reaction. She was prepared to quickly tuck the cub back into her bag if Page or Molly tried to chase it like they did Milquetoast. But much to Stacy's surprise, their reaction was one of curiosity instead of defensiveness. Stacy attributed this to the fact that the cub was so tiny and was a lynx instead of a house cat. (Page wouldn't want to get on the bad side of a lynx cub that could grow up to double Page's size and weight!) The dogs took turns sniffing the cub but then turned their attention to the wolves, wanting to greet each one and play with Wink.

Stacy walked into the cave and took a deep breath—it smelled of pine and was just as warm and comforting as she remembered it. She had missed it so much. Even though they'd only been on their Arctic expedition for about a week, it had felt like longer. So much had happened—the polar bear encounter, the narwhal rescue, meeting the elder wolf, rescuing the lynx cub, and surviving the avalanche—it felt much longer than just a week.

Stacy looked around for Milquetoast, but she didn't see him anywhere at first glance. She searched her bookcase—Fluff the chicken was there—but no Milquetoast. She looked inside the cave's fireplace, and near the back of the cave by the freshwater spring, and behind her rocking chair . . . but no Milquetoast. Stacy began to panic. She ran out of the cave into the clearing and called his name.

"Milquetoast!" Stacy said loudly. She didn't want to yell in case there were hikers nearby. "Milquetoast, come here!"

Page and Molly and the wolves came over to the bushes Stacy was searching.

"I can't find Milquetoast anywhere," Stacy said with a distraught tone. "He must have run away while we were gone!" *Where did he go? How long ago did he leave? What if a bear found him? Or worse, what if Droplet and Splat saw him and . . .* Stacy would never forgive herself for bringing the little cat into the taiga and then leaving him alone and defenseless; at least in the village he had been able to scrounge for scraps of food from the villagers. *Maybe he doesn't know how to hunt for mice! What if he starved?*

Stacy reached into her satchel and cradled the little cub. She was so looking forward to introducing it to Milquetoast—watching them grow and play together. And now that would never happen. The cub made a little squeak. The wolves all started looking in the bushes too. *Did he find his way back to the village? Is he looking for me? The wolves and I could mount a search party, combing through different parts of the taiga . . . maybe Milo and the other bats could help?*

Suddenly, a bark rang out from inside the cave. It was Addison. Stacy walked into the cave to where the wolf was standing.

"Addi, what?" Stacy said. She was still too upset about losing Milquetoast to care about what Addison needed her help with. She probably wanted to pore over one of the books in the cave to translate the runes or figure out what she should make the rest of the pack for dinner. Stacy walked over to her rocking chair but was tugged back by Addison, pulling at her sleeve. Addison led Stacy over to her clothes basket.

"Addison, I do *not* want to do laundry right now," Stacy said, turning back to her chair. "We'll go to the river tomorrow."

Purrrrrrrrr.

Stacy spun around. *Where is that sound coming from? It sounds exactly like a* . . . Stacy walked over to the clothes basket and peered inside. Stacy blinked—she couldn't believe it. Poking out from underneath Stacy's wadded-up flannel nightshirt was the tip of a black-and-gray-striped tail! Stacy lifted up the shirt and saw a cozy and curled-up Milquetoast . . . fast asleep.

"Oh, Milquetoast!" Stacy exclaimed, waking the cat up and lifting him out of the basket. "I thought I'd lost you." Milquetoast blinked his eyes and stretched in Stacy's arms. She set him down on the ground and pulled out the lynx cub from her bag and placed it on the ground beside Milquetoast. The cub let out another tiny squeak—it was too tiny to muster a proper meow. Milquetoast sniffed it apprehensively and then began to lick the cub's ears.

"He's grooming it!" Stacy exclaimed. She was so relieved that Milquetoast seemed to have accepted the cub. She also realized the cub needed a name. Stacy thought about the few things she knew so far about the cub and its personality. *We found it in the snow. It's very, very small. It's as quiet as a mouse, except for when it squeaks. . . .*

"Pipsqueak!" Stacy said suddenly. "We can call you Pip for short."

Milquetoast carried on grooming Pipsqueak for the next hour while Stacy and the pack settled back into life in the cave. Basil cleaned out the hearth and started a new fire with firewood that Wink and Everest carried in. Addison was cooking pumpkin stew for everyone's supper. Basil was sweeping out the cave and Noah was happily mopping the floor behind him. And Tucker was watching over everyone and helping out whenever he could. *Tucker is so sweet,* Stacy thought from over at her writing desk. *He's making sure that everyone is adjusting well to life in the cave with so many different animals here now.*

Stacy sat at her makeshift desk, trying to update her journal with everything that had happened on their expedition, but there was too much to write and her mind kept coming back to the runes and what they meant. She flipped back in her journal to the pages where she had drawn many of them from the ice cavern. Stacy was particularly drawn to the one that Addison had stood in front of for a long time. *This one is important. I just don't know what any of it means.*

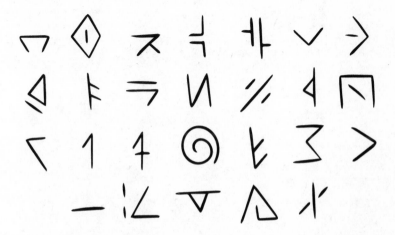

She pulled out her encyclopedia that had the entry about hieroglyphics, but just as Stacy thought, these did not look like them. Addison came over to where Stacy was sitting and rested her nose on Stacy's shoulder. Stacy looked for a long time at the symbols. She recognized some of them from the runes Addison saw on the tundra and the ones she found in the ice-spikes biome. *But these*

are different from the ones in the ice spikes because none of them repeat. All of them are unique—all . . . twenty-six of them. Wait a minute. There are twenty-six . . . just like . . . could it be? It is!

"Addison! It's the alphabet!"

TWENTY

STACY COULD NOT believe what she was looking at. The runes Addison had pointed out to her were a perfect match with the alphabet. It wasn't long before Stacy had written the corresponding letters next to each symbol and begun to translate the diary she'd taken from the glacier using the elder wolves' code. When she had completed several pages, she sat back and began to read.

> ~~I am a biologist.~~ I am an explorer. I am also a biologist, but I consider myself

an explorer first and foremost. That's what called me to the tundra in the first place. The thrill of terra incognita and the chance to live among what I consider the most ethereal animals in the world—the creatures of the Arctic. If you are reading this, then it is likely that you, like me, can walk with the ancient wolves of the north. Please keep my secret. It was a year into my expedition I learned of their existence. A new species. Not Arctic wolves—but rather, magical ~~otherworldly??~~ beings with powers. I don't know where the powers come from. Perhaps the heavens. Maybe even the aurora itself. But this much I know. Humankind cannot be trusted with the knowledge of their existence. It would be a spectacle, each wolf studied and prized for the different ability it possesses—maybe even hunted or abused as weapons of war. No. It will not happen. ~~As much as it disappoints me to exclude myself from the annals of discovery,~~ I will not take credit for their existence. No human should.

*What follows in the pages of this book is
a record of my findings during the years
I have spent and intend to spend yet with
these magnificent beings. This will include,
but is not limited to, my daily interactions
with them, my experiments and efforts to
extend their population beyond the current
breeding pair, and notes about the written
language I've developed with them and
taught them to use, which I write to you in
now. It is also a personal diary of my life
here with my partner, a talented artist who
graciously left his work behind to
live with me in secrecy. My life here is far
from conventional, but it is filled with
love, the pursuit of science, and daily
gratitude for the rare opportunity to live
and survive as a woman among these
"wolves."*

Stacy couldn't believe what she was reading. Her wolves were *not* Arctic wolves. Basil's lightning strike may have accelerated the development of her powers, but they hadn't *caused* them. Stacy's wolves had dormant powers because of their lineage, and they were brought to the taiga as pups. Addison probably picked up the rune language when she still lived with the elder wolves, since her ability was tied to intelligence. That's how she remembered it. *What happened to the explorer and her partner though? Why was the elder wolf all alone?* As much as she wanted to continue translating the journal, Stacy set it aside and worked well into the evening, decoding the runes in her notebook that she'd copied down from the cave walls. She hoped they would contain the answers to her questions. Addison brought a salmon en croute to Stacy at her writing desk so she could keep working. A few hours later, Basil came and lit a candle for Stacy. The ink in the pen Miriam had gifted Stacy was beginning to run dry and she had to retrace each word several times. The murals on the walls seemed to contain a history of the man and woman's time together in the glacier with the elder wolves. The last rune was giving Stacy problems, though. No matter which way she looked at it, she couldn't seem to make words out of the jumble of symbols.

She stared at it for a long time, until Everest came over to her and broke her concentration. Something about the way Everest looked at Stacy concerned her.

She picked up the candle and followed him as he led her to where Milquetoast and Pipsqueak were curled up together, cuddling.

"Aww," Stacy cooed. "Would you look at that. They're best friends."

Everest shook his head. He nudged Pipsqueak with his nose. The little lynx cub barely stirred. Everest nudged it harder. The lynx let out a little whimper but didn't open its eyes. Stacy scooped the cub up in her arms and examined it. It was underweight—Stacy already knew that. Stacy had been so preoccupied with decoding the runes that she hadn't paid any attention to how much dinner it ate.

"Has the cub been drinking?" Stacy asked around the cave, addressing the other wolves.

Noah stepped forward, a spoon in his mouth. It was clear he had been trying to get the cub to drink but hadn't been successful. Stacy became worried. She looked over at Tucker, who was sleeping by the fire. *His powers haven't returned yet. It could be days or weeks before they come back. What if they don't come back at all? What if Tucker's healing powers died along with the elder wolf?* Stacy turned to Everest.

"We all need to take turns watching Pipsqueak tonight," she said quietly. "Wake me up if its condition gets even worse."

Stacy's heart ached. She'd risked Everest's life (and her own) to rescue the lynx. They'd all survived the avalanche together. The thought that the cub might not make it through the night was unbearable. *We can't lose the cub. Milquetoast will be devastated. Tucker will blame himself for not being able to heal it. Pipsqueak was the silver lining to losing the elder wolf on the rescue expedition. If Pip dies, the whole expedition will feel like a failure. Just* then, Milo the bat flew into the cave and circled around Page, who then walked over to the map and pointed to the abandoned iron mine.

"A rescue?" Stacy asked. "Now?" This was the worst possible time for a rescue, but Stacy felt like they had no choice.

"Addison, you stay here and tend to Tucker," Stacy said. "Noah, you can take the first shift watching Pipsqueak. The others will come with me, including you, Page. Who knows if this animal is in an even worse state than Pip is. We have to see if we can help. We're rescuers, after all. Wild rescuers."

These words meant more to Stacy than ever before. Her wolves were meant to do this. They were the guardians of this taiga. All the wolves let out an enthusiastic bark in unison—clearly they were in agreement with her. Stacy said good-bye to Molly, Milquetoast, and especially to Pipsqueak. She hoped the cub would still be alive when she returned. Then she pulled on her leather boots, grabbed her bow and quiver of arrows, and ran after her magical wolves—out of the cave and into the dark, dark night.

STACY'S FAVORITE WORDS
FROM THE BOOK

adept—being very skilled or expert at something. Example: *Noah could breathe underwater just like the river fish he was so adept at catching.*

annals—a record of historical events. Example: *You'll be written in the annals of time for discovering a new species.*

chaos—a state of total confusion or lack of direction. Example: *If any of the reindeer saw a pack of wolves, they would panic, and chaos would erupt on the tundra.*

chortle—to laugh or chuckle. Example: *Stacy chortled at the sight of Everest teetering on a branch that looked like it might break at any moment.*

emanate—to come out or flow from a source. Example: *Heat began to emanate from Tucker's body, melting the snow around him and blanketing Stacy and the pack.*

ethereal—special or delicate in a way that feels other-worldly. Example: *The wolves are ethereal beings with powers.*

euphoric—having or feeling a state of intense happiness. Example: *A euphoric sense of relief washed over Stacy after they passed through the reindeer herd.*

floe—a flat piece of floating ice, known as an ice floe. Example: *The tundra broke off into miles and miles of ice floes that extended to the north and the east.*

forlorn—sad and lonely, or hopeless. Example: *Tucker's forlorn howl filled Stacy with sudden dread.*

frolic—to play or romp around cheerfully. Example: *While the wolves frolicked in the evening light, Stacy sat down on a boulder and sketched the sunset.*

gargantuan—gigantic in size. Example: *Inside the glacier was a gargantuan ice cavern.*

incredulous—unwilling to believe something; doubtful. Example: *Stacy was incredulous that Addison could read the ice runes.*

kerfuffle—a commotion. Example: *The cat's tail hairs stood on end and doubled in size during the kerfuffle.*

milquetoast—a timid and meek person (or animal). Example: *Milquetoast was a very milquetoast cat.*

mottled—having blotchy or spotted coloring. Example: *Droplet and Splat had dark coats mottled with patches of brown, black, and gray.*

ominous—threatening in appearance. Example: *Stacy awoke and saw the ominous ice spikes looming in the distance.*

ornery—unhappy, pouty, or unpleasant. Example: *They had yet to see any other signs of life aside from the snowshoe hares and one ornery marmot that wanted nothing to do with them.*

palatial—spacious and impressive; palace-like. Example: *The cavern was both glacial and palatial.*

pandemonium—a wild uproar; chaos. Example: *Suddenly, pandemonium erupted inside the cave.*

pang—a sudden feeling of sorrow or pain. Example: *A sudden pang of sadness washed over Stacy at the thought of leaving this magical place.*

pristine—something that is like new or clean and untouched. Example: *The tundra was untouched and pristine—just waiting to be explored.*

relinquish—to let go or surrender control. Example: *Everest relinquished his grip on Norman's tusk.*

reverberate—to create a series of echoes. Example: *Tucker let out a sorrowful howl that reverberated through the glacier walls.*

ricochet—to bounce around or rebound. Example: *Milquetoast ricocheted around the cave, searching desperately for a safe place to hide.*

studious—interested in learning and studying. Example: *Addison was Stacy's most studious wolf.*

swath—a large patch of grass or land. Example: *The mesa biome had flat swaths of sage and cactus that stretched as far as the eye could see.*

terra incognita—undiscovered or unexplored territory. Example: *Stacy wondered if the ice-spikes biome was terra incognita.*

tinge—slight bit of color. Example: *Addison's coat had tinges of brown and rust red.*

trepidation—a nervous or uncertain feeling. Example: *Stacy noted a slight sense of trepidation in Everest's movements.*

unscathed—uninjured; without a scratch. Example: *Stacy knew Wink could survive falling into the ice unscathed.*

MEET THE REAL-LIFE MILQUETOAST!

Stacy found Milquetoast in a grocery store parking lot in the winter of 2015. He was a cold, malnourished, and injured stray cat. Stacy had to coax him out of his hiding spot with fish treats—much like how you tame an ocelot in Minecraft! The funny thing is . . . Stacy had a Siamese cat in her Dogcraft world named Milquetoast for over a year before she found him in real life!

Breed: Lilac Lynx Point Siamese

Age: Unknown (approximately five years old)

Rescue date: November 18, 2015

Favorite activity: Being held like a baby by Stacy

Favorite foods: Tuna, pumpkin

Fun fact: Milquetoast has caught several mice at Stacy's cabin and can be quite ferocious despite his name!

GET TO KNOW A BEAR BIOLOGIST!

The behavior of the animals in *Wild Rescuers: Expedition on the Tundra* is fantasy. To learn more about the real animals of the Arctic, Stacy was able to interview a bear biologist!

Name:
Wes Larson

Current job:
Wildlife biologist

How did you get the nickname "Griz Kid"?
I gave it to myself when I picked an Instagram name! I knew I wanted to work with bears, and I also love University of Montana football (the Montana Griz!).

Wes Larson next to an abandoned polar bear den in Alaska.

What's it like working on the tundra and in the Arctic?
EXTREMELY COLD. All of my trips to the

Arctic have been during the winter, when it can regularly get down to -50 or -60 degrees Fahrenheit. There aren't any trees or plants, and everything is covered by snow and ice. It's incredibly flat, so it almost feels like you are on another planet—an endless flat, white spread of snow and ice. It's incredible that polar bears and other animals can survive there! We humans need to bundle up with the best gear available in order to avoid freezing to death.

What wildlife have you encountered on your expeditions?
On my expeditions to the Arctic, I have encountered polar bears, Arctic fox, Arctic wolves, caribou, musk oxen, snowy owls, red fox, lemmings, ptarmigan, and a few other species!

How do you locate abandoned polar bear dens?
Abandoned dens are much easier to find than occupied dens because there are generally tracks leading away from the den and sometimes an open hole in the snowdrift. Occupied dens are much harder to find as the bear digs into the snowdrift, and then it snows over the hole that she

has dug. We use infrared cameras or dog teams to find those dens. In the best case scenario, we have a bear that has a GPS collar, and then we can simply use our GPS and radio receiver and antenna to track her to her den. Once we find the bears, we set up a camera to record them leaving the den as well as the behavior of the adult bear and her cubs. These videos give us important information that helps us learn about the behavior of denning bears and how we can best avoid disturbing them during a critical and vulnerable part of their lives.

What advice would you give to young people who want to work in your field?

Don't give up! Getting into a wildlife program in college can be tricky and sometimes takes a lot of persistence. Volunteer on as many projects as you possibly can in your area and then, once you find the college program you want to be in, make sure you keep trying to get in! It may take years, but that kind of persistence usually pays off! Also, remember that wildlife biologists usually still spend a lot of their time inside writing and reading, so don't become a wildlife biologist if you want a job that will have you outside every day!

How can we help the polar bears?

Do your best to conserve energy however you can! Plant trees, avoid waste like single-use plastics, ride a bike instead of driving a car, and most important, encourage your parents to vote for politicians who care about the environment! And if you are old enough to vote, make sure to vote for people who want to save our wildlife!

About Griz Kid:

Wes "Griz Kid" Larson has been working with both black bears and polar bears for the last eight years. He also hosts an online show, *Mission*

Wild, where he travels the world and learns about other wildlife biologists and their projects. He has worked with African wild dogs, pangolins, American alligators, hawks, eagles, elephant seals, tejus, and a ton of other animals. He loves being a wildlife biologist! You can follow his adventures at Instagram.com/GrizKid.

ACKNOWLEDGMENTS

Thank you to my editor, David Linker, as well as Camille Kellogg, Mitchell Thorpe, Vaishali Nayak, and everyone I work with at HarperCollins, including Caitlin Garing and Almeda Beynon. And Zane Birdwell from John Marshall Media and Mario Crystal from MetCom Studios for their excellent work on my audiobooks.

Thank you, Jessie Gang, for another beautiful book—you're just my favorite. And five million thank-yous to Wild Rescuers's illustrator Vivienne To—receiving your covers and illustrations for my books is better than Christmas morning.

Thank you to my mom for your creative ideas and keen typo-finding skills and to my dad for everything you've done for my merchandise endeavors and also for your endless enthusiasm for my wolf pack (specifically Everest!). Thank you to Madeline Lansbury—for many things, but most importantly for drawing the wonderful symbol alphabet and runes that appear in this book and managing all my author events.

Thank you to my YouTube family who I love so much: Joe, Beth, Lizzie, Joel, Delly, Alexa, Kat, Allen, Kim, Betty, Wenny, Tiff, and Mario. And, last but most certainly not least, thank you to my YouTube subscribers, many of whom I got to meet on tour for this book series. I love you all SO MUCH! Page and Molly love you; go rescue a dog.